E.V.P.

Short for Electronic
Voice Phenomena.
The process of contacting
the deceased with
electronic entertainment
devices.

THE ELECTRONIC GHOSTS

Paperback new edition

NATHAN TOMS

Disguise Books

Disguise Books

Nathan Toms asserts the moral rights to be identified as the author of this work.

Printed and bound in the USA

© N. P. Toms 2001

First Published in 2004 by Disguise Books/LULU press Inc

ISBN 1438226608 ISBN:13 9781438226606

New paperback edition re-revised 2008. This edition published by Disguise Books in arrangement with Velvet Books, United Kingdom

www.mysterydisguise.co.uk

Thank you to Angela, Jason, and Janet in helping with the editing for my book.

Table Of Contents

The Electronic Ghosts

Preface

Written By Nathan Toms, October 2003

This story contains many social aspects, especially the first part about people's interest on what may become of them when they finally die. This leads on into the second part of my story of one man's involvement and experiments with 'Electronic Voice Phenomena', 'Spiricom', and contacting deceased people using the methods of tape machines, radios, videos, and other electronic devices.

We follow the man Andrew Stein from his early life, his meeting with many characters and events sending him on a discovery into the world of the 'Paranormal' and the 'Unexplained', and the drama and episodes that are connected with this subject.

My influences for my story I will go into briefly. I would like to thank the many *authors* of fascinating books written in precise scientific detail about the subjects of 'Electronic Voice Phenomena' and 'Spiricom'. Although my story is completely fictitious, with sublime fantasy notions thrown in, I do like to think that I have been favourable with my story in some aspects of this unexplained science.

Konstantin Raudive's book *Breakthrough* is a masterpiece of information, which gave me the initial inspiration to write this book.

In addition, George W Meek and William O Neil's *Spiricom* machine that they built to contact a Dr. Mueller - gave me other ideas to liven up my manuscript.

ITC is short for 'Instrumental Transcommunication'. A method of using video evidence and sound samples for proof, if any is needed, that there are people who have passed on to the other side and are making direct visual and audible conversations with the living - and this subject figures later in my story.

Now my own interest in this topic came about by accident when I stumbled upon Raudive's book: *Breakthrough An Amazing Experiment In Contacting The Dead* while in my local library. That was back in 1993. Consequently I began my own research and obtained results from 'E.V.P. Spirit Voices' addressing me by 'name.' I came to the conclusion that this science is genuine. But I hasten to add I am not sure from what source these spirit voices come from. This always stuck in my mind after getting E.V.P. voices back which became menacing in tone, this influenced my story greatly to create a character to reflect this.

After reading in more detail Raudive's book in the days before I commenced writing my own story, the quotations he wrote down purporting to come from various famous, and notorious figures of world history, rested uneasy on my mind. The question is: *Are these genuine people who have died giving out comfort to their relatives, proclaiming they still exist in some form or another. Or are they malevolent entities fooling the researchers who are contacting them?*

Dr. Konstantin Raudive pioneer of EVP

The man who gave me the inspiration to write this book

Man has an inherent, stubborn characteristic: the wish to fathom his own destiny-within himself and concerning himself. We die whilst we live, for our concepts of life and death conceal the future that awaits us.

'Dr. Konstantin Raudive'

1906-1974

*For the special friends in the world
unseen*

PROLOGUE

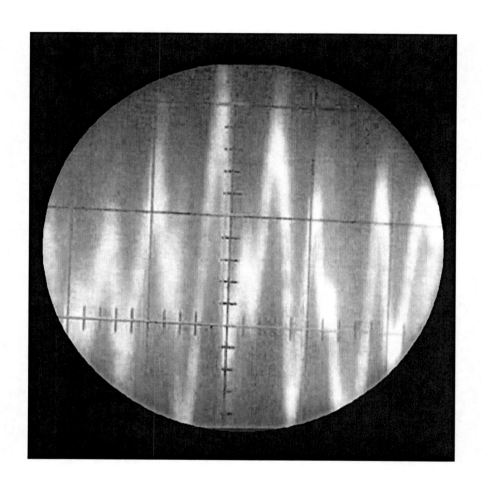

The 1980s

I was standing in my ravaged and fire damaged house hallway, with numerous electronic devices and other items lying partly burnt, and destroyed. The mess disheartened me immensely. It had been a cloudy miserable day outside which contributed to the depression I greatly felt. The boarded up front door began slamming open and shut due too the mischievous wind and the pungent smell of soot filled my nostrils and polluted the air. I took a few steps forward stepping over a television set that had been burnt and cracked open, due to heat - an oscilloscope, plus another burnt out device lay scattered across a large blackened table. I went to the kitchen and observed the terrible mess. The electric cooker lay on its side, and other kitchen items were strewn smashed and broken on the tiled ground - while two knives were still embedded in the far wall. I waited for a moment before I turned around to check somewhere else out. I now stood at the bottom of the staircase, burnt out video cameras were still positioned up the wall, as they had been nine months earlier. The stairs had sustained too much damage for me to be able to get up them. I shook my head and let out a groan of displeasure. I then slowly entered the living room. Smashed ornaments greeted my eyes as I looked down to the charred carpet floor, it seemed to be still wet due to water damage caused by the pipes of the radiators leaking. Next I made my way over to the dining table. Numerous pieces of paper and other documents rested on top of it. I fumbled my way through the mess on the table and pulled out a partly burnt, thick book. The book's title was called, *Breakthrough An Amazing Experiment To Contact Voices From The Dead*. It stood out due to its gold lettering. I blew some of the ash off it, which caused some pages to fall out and I flicked through the inside of this literature - but most of the book seemed barely recognizable due to having been so badly burnt. Suddenly I felt an icy shiver come over me, I put the book back on the dining table and my eyes glanced around the living room again. There had been hardly any daylight coming through from the windows, as they were all boarded up leaving only a small chink of light to come from one of the boarded up openings. This gave my surroundings the aura of an Egyptian tomb. I stood in a solemn reflective fashion and my mood rested heavy on my already shaken mind.

The terrible events that had happened in the house, without question had brought about my own foolish downfall. One man's untimely death was caused by the events that had unfolded. I questioned my own reason and sanity on what I'd unfortunately instigated. I'd dabbled with something from the paranormal unknown. At first things seemed remarkable, but as time went on I had unleashed a force that not only addicted me to continue further, but also frightened Anna my wife, Michael my friend, and inevitably myself. I still did not even know if this ghostly entity Natasha would one day make an unwelcome return.

When I lay on that accident and emergency table near to death I had come to see visions that could not be explained. For the first time in my life I feared death, not of any of the myths that surrounded it, but a feeling of being detached from this earthly life, knowing that none of your closest loved ones could ever see you, or hear you in a physical form.

The causes of our quest to know of what becomes of us when we die, and the proof that is needed to convince the many skeptics, psychiatrists and scientists that there really is some kind of energy that survives, when the mortal body and brain ceases to function anymore seems paramount to many parts of the human race.

I thought that *The Electronic Voice Phenomena and Spiricom*, the process of making specific complicated electronic machines could have been a way to contact this realm where we are all supposed to go. That could have been the answer to my desires.... As a young man I relentlessly dabbled into everything. I had been a product of the sixties' decade, the drugs, music and the clothes were experienced thoroughly by myself. I never attained any prominent views at all about ghosts or ever wanting to contact them, in my opinion it just seemed mumbo jumbo and a weirdo's paradise. I suppose when I served in the army in the early 1960s these ideas did not interest me. But they should have, as I had witnessed fellow army comrades die painfully, so maybe I ought to have become more informed, especially after the death of the old man Stan I dealt with back in 'Civvy Street.'

The *Stan* character is also a major point to my story as he was a part of my youth. When you're young you think the routine of the forthcoming years will see you live out the normal society values of a stable fulfilling life, but unforeseen occurrences can put paid to this. My first marriage represented this, and broke up mainly due to my selfish foolish moods. But luckily fortune did smile on me as marriage to my second wife Anna followed a few years later, however, after the recent turbulent adventure I had put her through it's amazing she has stayed with me. So as a consequence readers, I think it best to commence the first part of my story, starting from the swinging sixties.

Chapter 1

The Early 1960s

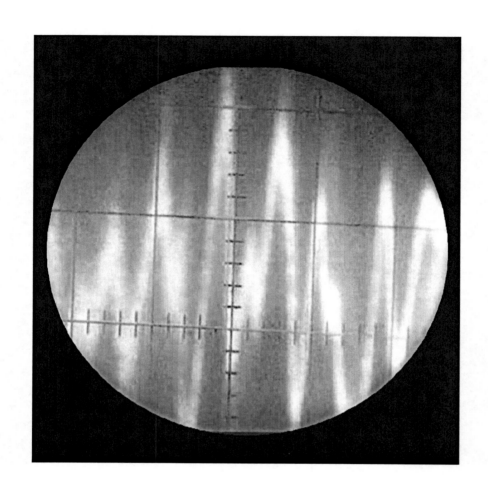

1960s

I waited nervously outside the British army's office room. I then glimpsed at my watch before peering through the door slit. I could see the clerk sitting at his tatty wooden desk preparing to sign my discharge papers for me to leave the army. He shouted my name and I accordingly knocked on the office door – marching in confidently. The army clerk glanced up at me with indifference then passed the discharge papers.

'Would you mind signing here Stein?' Angry military shouting came from outside on the parade ground, this distracted my attention briefly before the army clerk cleared his throat to bring me round to complete my final task.

'Oh sorry, yes sir,' I replied with a slight stutter in my voice. I signed the papers with my *Hollywood star signature* and with expectation I prepared to march out, obviously the army clerk had to have a final sarcastic comment. 'Good luck in civvy street Stein. You're gonna need it!' He gave a sly slow smile as I left his office.

Outside I took a deep breath and continued along the corridor on my way to freedom, my mind pondering in thought. 'God knows what I'm going to do now. Anyway I can't complain, seeing I've had a free holiday round many different countries, with the help of her majesty's pound and the sergeant major's boot implanted up my arse!'

At the railway station in town I purchased a second-class ticket to *Kings Cross* in London and made my way towards platform seven. The environment at the station was quiet, pacing up and down impatiently my freshly shined army shoes made a grinding noise on the rough concrete. Due to fatigue I decided to sit down on one of the seats, which graced the platform. I took out from my green trouser pocket a freshly rolled cigarette, before striking a match on the floor to ignite it. Taking a long deep puff I spoke quietly to myself letting out my inner questions:

'My stepfather is going to be really pleased to see me. He wanted me to stay in the army, but why should I. I have done my four years of Infantry service. I'm in the big wide world now and it's up to me to do something. I want to experience the sixties' revolution and liberation. These times of fashionable clothes, the music and the events that are happening in this fantastic period of freedom.' I coughed a bit as some smoke from the cigarette I was gasping went down the wrong way. Minutes past, then the sound of my train approached and pulled juddering into the station. I stood up, lifted my cases and got onto the train. A few of the carriages doors slammed shut in an erratic fashion. The train jerked slightly and my journey commenced back home taking me inevitably towards Civvy Street.

Further into the journey we passed through Leicester, Loughborough and numerous other towns and cities. Wiping the condensation from the dirty carriage window I peered outside through the cloudy blur with a thoughtful expression, unaware of what would happen when I arrived back at my stepfather's house. My eyes waned heavy, as tired - I drifted into a pained sleep.

'Pound will that do?' I said, while I reached into my pocket for my half empty wallet to pay the taxi fare.

'Yeah son that's fine,' replied the cabbie in his cockney accent. Money was exchanged and off sped the taxi. Then I stood by the gate of my stepfather's house. The cunning fool had obviously been watching me because he opened the front door to the house before I had time to knock. His face was agitated, as was his brash manner.

'Ah so you're back! Come crawling like a gutless waster. Just couldn't take it then. Eh? Get in now!' he said. I approached angrily pushing my way past the idiot, this made him stumble back nearly knocking into the ornate cabinet as I entered into the house.

'That's a nice bloody welcome in it,' I angrily retorted. 'Thanks for your grateful support. What would I do without you.'

I now stood in the hallway. The heavy front door then came crashing shut. I spun around shocked. My stepfather's temper was now rising. 'Come here varmint!' he screamed.

'For Christ sake what's your problem? I have been on the damn train for the last eight hours.'

My stepfather's *eyes* widened, he also was gritting his teeth, plus the stench of alcohol oozed from his breath as flaming poison. 'If you think that you are living with me than you are in for a surprise,' he said. 'You have to make your own way in the world now. I don't want you living with your mother and me. When you went in the army to do your service you had a good chance to make a career for yourself, but now you have thrown it all away.'

I was now feeling the urge to pound him with a left hook. I moved my left fist closer into range of his face and my posture and tone was now at boiling point. 'I've done my bit for *Queen and Country*, that's enough,' I shot back. 'Y'know I'm sick of this. I've only just got through the front door and you've started. On and on you go like a rabbit. You've the mindset of a *poxy* mynah bird. Save the perverted crap on how to live a life, as your life experience resides in the bottom of a whisky bottle!' Abruptly my stepfather gripped my shirt and yelled louder. 'If you think you are going to be one of these idle bastards who listen to the Who,

Beatles, Rolling Stones and the Monkees with that dreadful shit music they all sell, and ride around on motorbikes and scooters fighting—' I then interrupted his mad raving by slamming my heavy suitcase down hard onto my stepfather's foot with a lot of force. He began screaming with pain as he released me from his grip. 'Oh Christ my foot!' He bent down to touch it, 'you've broken my *bleedin'* foot!' My eyes were now greeted with the hilarious sight of my stepfather hopping about on one foot, he resembled a character from a 'Loony Tunes' cartoon I watched as a kid, but I could not remember the name of it for the life of me.

My mother's voice could then be heard shouting downstairs. 'Barry what on earth is going on down there?'

My vocal chords went into untamed laughter. 'I'm so sorry Barry.' I had a delightful glee of revenge at this man's agony. My stepfather was now standing painfully, he paused, cursed, then loud and abrupt he shouted. 'Right that settles it...out you go tomorrow, bag and baggage! Yer get me!'

My mother came down the stairs, spoke a brief passing comment to me and then helped my stepfather Barry walk slowly to the kitchen. She made him sit on a wooden stool and slowly and carefully he took off his shoe and sock from his painful right foot before he cursed in agony. *Now you see my stepfather had never been the diplomat. I suppose ever since when I caught him a few years ago with his trousers round his ankles and giving the vicar's daughter Maisy a good seeing to. It's amazing, even when I caught him in the act he denied it, just saying he was practicing a new kind of first aid technique.* Well that's my stepfather for you - just a king sized wanker. He ruled my mother *Cecilia* with lies and deceit, ever since she married him four years ago on the rebound from the death of my real father who died in Korea. She never came to terms with it and sided with everything my stepfather done. I wish my real father were still alive, he would never have treated me in this awful pig shot way.

Later on I was wandering about town when the sound and smells of a pub: *The King George* drew my thirsty being into its doors. It appeared not to be too busy. An elderly man sat in the corner and briefly caught my *eye*. My feet that were encased in my black army boots moved in military fashion towards the bar-counter and I asked the Barman for a 'drink.' He looked into my eyes with an untrustworthy expression. 'What are you drinking?'

'Give me a pint please of your best bitter!' My breath sighed and my fingers began tapping on the varnished wooden counter as this person did my beverage. He then put the glass down hard in front of me. 'There you go,' he said. I gave the money for the drink and took a few sips. It tasted very good and I certainly needed a drink after the events of the day. The Barman huffed and subsequently stepped away.

Throughout the early evening I downed a couple of pints gazing aimlessly around the bar for female companionship.

'Hey son have you got a light?' came an old man's voice. Startled I turned around and noticed the *same* elderly gentleman who I caught a glimpse of when I first entered into the pub. I was about to have my first encounter with the old man Stan. Walking over to him I struck a match and I gave him the light for his pipe while not saying a word. Stan curiously asked, 'Not got much to say for yourself son. What's up? You look like you have got the whole world on your shoulders.'

'Why should you care,' I said, with a soft voice as I sat down opposite the old man. 'No one has spoken to me all night, there isn't even any decent woman in here to chat up.'

Stan patted me on the shoulder and said, 'Well I'm talking to you.' He then took a puff from his pipe.

I looked intently at him. 'So what, you're just an old man probably going to lecture me on the good old days. You lot are all the same.'

Stan countered back with his answer. 'No I am not...I'm just trying to make conversation with you.' He pointed his tobacco stained finger at me like a pistol and continued with his rant. 'Now I will tell you to your face what I think of you. I speak my mind how it is, and how god's will has it written.' He began raising his voice. 'Maybe that's why I don't have any bloody friends.' The Barman glanced over towards where Stan and me were sitting with disdain.

The old man continued to speak out his patronizing sentence. 'Drunk or sober, you will know exactly how I will feel about you.' After finishing his words he supped his pint and sucked on his *Sherlock Holmes* style pipe. I gazed at him with slight amusement thinking: *What am I sitting here talking to this stupid old man for.* I prepared to get up as I found his conversation irritating. Suddenly Stan grabbed my arm:

'You're in trouble son,' his tone changed to concern. 'I can tell, what's wrong?'

I replied back to him a bit apologetic. 'Well, I'm not normally like this. I'm just really pissed off. Done my army service, seen the world - and been to places I have only dreamed about. So now that I've left the army I thought life can only get better.'

'So what's up army boy?' asked Stan.

'It's my stepfather! He wanted me to stay in the army after my four-year *contract*, but I'd had enough. I wish now that maybe I should of stayed in if this is what civilian life is going to be like.' My tone became angrier, 'Seeing the fat bastard has now thrown me out. I only got back today. A few hours ago, and we had a massive row, now he has thrown me out, and told me to find somewhere else to live!'

'Mmm,' Stan chuckled a bit in response.

I did not see the joke and replied back. 'What's funny?'

Stan scratched his baldhead. 'You are!'

'Why, why am,' I asked?

Stan philosophically came back with his answer. 'So much of your life left to live. What have I got to look forward to.' There followed a thoughtful pause before he spoke with a slow move of words from his mouth: '...The Grave...'

Stan put his hand into his pocket and pulled some old coins out. 'Go and get two pints,' he asked, 'by the way, what name do you go by son?' Stan turned his ear towards me.

'Andrew Stein,' I replied, 'by the way, what's your name old man?'

'Just call me Stan.' He put his greasy palm out and we shook hands slightly.

At the bar I held my finger up and pointed to the Barman to give me two pints. The Barman was flushed and coarse. 'Hang on. I've only got one pair of hands!' he moaned back. 'I'm busy doing drinks.'

Impatiently my eyes made 'blatant signals' to him. 'Come on!' I protested, but the Barman had other things on his mind, he was serving these two young ladies and gazed lovingly at them, 'What will you have Miss,' he asked in a fanciful tone. He then continued being a creep with his banter. 'And say, maybe later, is there anything else I will be able to do - for you two attractive beauties?'

My attention became distracted as I saw a few more people enter into this public house. A drunken couple with a woman having one of those loud cringing laughs left through the entrance. Then various sounds of laughter, merriment and talking filled the place. Looking back at the Barman he seemed to be having a spot of trouble with the two women he was attending to. One of whom, had an irritating stuck up posh voice. 'A gin and tonic, and one vodka with a slim line tonic I specifically said.'

However, the Barman had mistakenly cocked up the drinks by putting a normal tonic in the vodkas. He then placed the drinks in front of the ladies. The outcome was inevitable. The women gave the Barman a snobby look at the drinks he'd prepared and then in an arrogant voice one of them said:

'I'm not drinking that! It's got a normal tonic in it...I expressly asked for a slim line tonic.' The Barman and one of the women continued arguing for a few minutes and these were the words I could hear through the noise of the pub's din.

Irritated words were spoken.

'Oh come on! It does not matter.'

'I want a slim line tonic in my vodka.'

'Come on, oh please?' 'No! It's not on. I don't need this shit. Bollocks you tart!' This went on for a few minutes more and then the two women brushed past me to obviously leave. The Barman had prepared some new drinks, putting them firmly on the bar counter.

'Where are they now?' he asked me.

'Well can't you see they are leaving,' I replied as I pointed my hand in the direction of the two women.

'Hey!' he screamed, but it was too late, they'd left, slamming the pub door quite hard. The Barman who by the sight of him had obviously been having a bad day shouted in their direction:

'Flaming stuck up - stinking stupid slags!' His posture was getting enraged with his skin turning red with anger. 'Bloody lousy slags! I hate this job - idiots wasting my time...Idiots! This job is a load of bollocks.' He continued cursing repeatedly like a scratched record, shook his head in disgust, and his eyes were scowling when finally he turned to me. 'It was two pints of bitter you wanted?'

'Yes please,' I replied in a timid voice trying not to wind him up anymore. 'I hope you haven't been too inconvenienced by my order?' The Barman wheezed and began grumbling to himself as he was doing my drinks. Next he slammed them down in front of me, then lent across the bar as I gave him the money. Speaking quietly and nosily into my ear he spoke some words to me. 'I could not help in noticing you sitting over in the corner and talking to Stan,' he said with slyness in his voice. 'If you take my advice you will stay well away from him.' He gave a sneering glance in Stan's direction.

'Why,' I asked a bit puzzled.

'Because he's *er* crazy old man. His mind is pickled with alcohol, causing him to tell make believe nonsense stories, that are unbelievable to a rational man. What with him and his fat old mad sister he's shacked up with.'

'Is he not married then?' I asked with doubt. The Barman stood back away and began emptying the ashtrays. 'Course he isn't,' he said with disdain. 'Who do you think would put up with him?'

'You're slightly judgmental aren't you,' I quipped.

'Oh piss off!' came the Barman's swift reply - before he moved away to serve another customer.

As I sat back down opposite Stan with our drinks the old man quipped:

'Trouble with *Ted* the Barman?'

'Nothing I cannot handle,' I said, 'he seems to get very impatient with people.'

Stan took a sip from his pint and smiled. 'Well now son I was in the military for twelve years.'

'Were you?' I said suspiciously. Stan then told me his story, I did not know if it was true or not but kept my opinions to myself. Apparently when he was a young man about eighteen, his father and mother sent him out to get some paraffin and other items, but while on the way there, for some reason he did not specify, he somehow decided to drop into the local Army Recruiting Centre, and signed the papers to join up and receive the *King's* shilling. Things must have been very different in the early nineteen hundreds, a speedy medical examination, and bingo he was off to of all places: India! Funny I thought, 'where did he spend his embarkation leave before sailing to India.' I thought it best not to ask. He then studiously continued with his story. Apparently after a number of years spent in the various countries he returned home and was greeted by theses words sarcastically from his family:

'Where the blazes have you been? You've been away donkey's years for our winter fuel Stan?' For some reason this became a sort of family yarn, long after his homecoming.

After a couple of minutes I began to look at Stan's face and examined its many defects. The only hair he'd got left on his scalp - was two little tufts sticking out from the vicinity above his ears. He moaned that in the summer the top of his head became like a glass like surface. It unfortunately made a good skating rink for pesky flies and other insects that are attracted to baldheads. I then noticed a big white handkerchief hanging out of Stan's top pocket. 'Is that what that accessory is used for?' I inquired.

'Yes,' replied Stan jokingly. 'It comes into use, with repetitive swipes to brush the insects off.'

I looked even more closely at Stan's face, which triggered some mild amusement. It had a rather compressed, nay bulldog expression to it. You could say it had the features of someone who had been chewing a wasp. I articulated this fact to him not wanting the old man to take this in offence. In response, Stan brushed his left hand down his face slowly and spoke uptight.

'Yes I know. It's the eons of time that has done this to it.'

I lit up a cigarette, and took a deep puff, while doing this I also noticed Stan's nose had a big dent in it that made it turn upwards.

'How an earth did you manage to do that to your nose?' I asked.

Stan was now starting to get aggravated. 'Right! Are you going to slag me off about my face all night. You aren't a pretty picture yourself.'

Putting my hand through my cropped hair I replied in jest. 'Yeah, but at least I've still got this on my scalp Stan.'

Stan regained his composure and explained to me that his nose got broken when his sister Glad dropped him as an infant on one of those cast iron gates that were commonplace in most properties in the late nineteenth century. I asked Stan 'where his sister Glad lived now.' He explained after first taking out his handkerchief to wipe the top of his shiny head - apparently she lived with him, at their house they owned. He stated proudly that it was not much, but it suited the two of them just fine, she took care of his needs and kept the place tidy. I suspected he might be getting bored with our conversation as he opened his mouth to yawn. I noticed the only teeth Stan had left were a few protruding from his lower jaw.

'What an earth do you use those teeth you have got left for?' I said.

He closed his mouth quickly and said, 'Their sole purpose is to support my beloved pipe.' He put the pipe in his mouth with majestic expression acting as if he was the *King of England*. The way he was sucking on it reminded me of baby with a dummy in its mouth. After a lingering pause Stan posed a serious question to me:

'Now Andrew, you say that you have nowhere to live, and have been chucked out of your parents home. Well at the moment I've got a spare room to let with my sister Glad and me. You are quite—' Stan was rudely interrupted by the pub's main door suddenly being banged open, and in walked a heavy rough looking man, who by the sight of him resembled a *criminal docker*. He was like one of those people you did not want to bump into down a dark road one night, to add insult to injury he ripped the power chord from the flashing jukebox. The Docker shouted angrily and seemed obviously after trouble. 'Who was the piece of shit? Who called my wife a slag, when she tried to get a drink!' The whole bar became quiet. There was a lot of murmuring from the customers; I knew the Barman must be the poor soul who was going to face the wrath of this individual.

Subsequently, me with Stan sitting opposite turned and looked in the direction of Ted the Barman, so did a few other customers. Two other shady looking men then followed the Docker through the pub's entrance; they both gave menacing eye-to-eye contact with a few people before they stopped. Next some extra people *pointed* in the direction of the Barman. The Docker saw this and stomped over to the bar where Ted was serving. The Docker banged his fist hard on the counter and yelled, 'You're the bastard who gave my wife the wrong drink! And called her a slag!'

'That's right,' replied the Barman in a cocky tone. 'She deserved it. For wasting my time!' The Barman moved himself closer, so that his eyes came into contact with the Docker's unshaven face. This action caused a couple of drinks on the counter to fall over and spill their liquid contents.

'Oh no here we go again,' muttered Stan as he put his head in his hands.

'What, what do you mean?' I whispered with a bit of a stammer. The mayhem then kicked off. There were glasses being thrown causing them to smash and gripping and slapping sounds were heard. Then in an instant the Docker pulled the Barman over the counter and started pushing and shoving him about. A few tables were knocked over and a *man* tried to break up the fight, his unjustified reward for this was to get a hard punch in the face by the Docker causing this unfortunate individual to fall onto the table where myself and Stan were sitting causing our drinks, plus Stan's pipe to go flying in opposite directions. A couple of woman 'screamed' in a hysterical manner. The Barman threw punches in quick succession, but the Docker brushed them away with the ease of a heavyweight boxer. After that, the Docker held the Barman in a headlock and was hitting him. Both of them staggered about, shouts were heard and more tables fell over. The two shady characters that followed the Docker in then got involved. Glasses and all other kinds of items went travelling throughout the air, and the sound of punches and dull thuds, with their direct impact became louder. The bar now resembled a seventeenth century gin house complete with lawlessness.

Stan dug his bony tobacco stained finger into my arm and said, 'Quick we are leaving.' We both got up trying to make our way to the pub door. But the struggling Barman and Docker came alarmingly toward us, knocking into myself - this incensed me and I violently pushed out at them, they both staggered backwards and fell over an upturned table into the laps of some unfortunate locals. Woman's voices in the pub screamed in semaphore:

'For Gawd sake! Someone call the police! These lunatics are wrecking the place.'

Stan and me somehow made it outside to the front of the public house. Nevertheless, to my further concerns the lawlessness was becoming increasingly out of control inside this awful drinking den and Ale and wine glasses, plus other objects were flying about and cracking against the interior. I asked Stan while trying to regain my breath, 'I did think, that this was a quiet pub, and maybe respectable?'

Stan brushed himself down and replied, 'Course it isn't. Why do you think I go in there for! You don't get no quiet life in there.'

'Yes but I thought—' I was stopped from speaking another word by the shattering of glass, and the strange sight of the Barman coming hurtling through the main bar window. He hit the ground with a dull thud and landed dazed and bloodstained on the pavement, with myself, and the cynical facial features of Stan looking over him. The Barman was groaning and moaning which I suppose was to be expected.

'Oh…ah. Owl. Ohh!' he cried. Stan walked around this poor soul in slow fashion, stood over him, eyed him up and down, laughed, and then for some strange reason made a sucking noise from his lungs and mouth - then with spiteful venom spat some black stained mucus onto the Barman's forehead. I was astonished by Stan's lack of sympathy. The Barman's eyes flickered open and gritting his crooked teeth he screamed, 'Why you! Bastard filthy scumbag! I'll KILL YOU! Do you hear me! I will tear your head off and shit down your…' I took a hold of Stan's brown jacket and thought it best to make an escape before this raging wild animal of a human being killed both of us. We both trotted off quickly down the road, as a police bell was heard approaching in the distance.

'Come on Stan?' I protested while pulling him along the road. The old man was chuckling to himself with glee.

I spoke to him astonished. 'Why on earth did you spit on his head for, you know he was pissed off?'

'He deserved it,' replied Stan while taking a couple of deep breaths. 'He's never liked me, since I told him to his face what an arrogant swine he be!' Stan was coughing heavily due to the exertion of our long run. After a few more exchanges he again asked me 'did I want to rent the spare room in his house he shared with his sister Glad?' With alcohol and the previous events of the evening clouding my proper judgment, and with nowhere else to go after tomorrow I accepted his offer. The address was *24 Runcorn Road*; I was given instructions of where to find it. I was to come around about two o clock in the afternoon and he told me that he would get Glad to get my room prepared for me when I arrived. After saying our goodbyes Stan began making his own way back to his place of abode.

Consequently I prepared to return to my stepfather's house as soon as possible, pack my stuff, and early in the next morning be on my way.

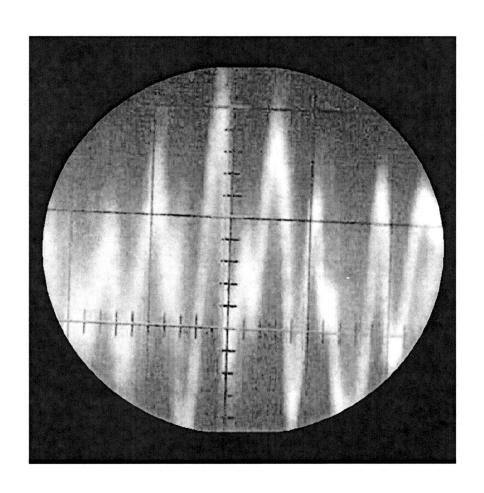

Chapter 2

Eccentric Personalities

It was now two o clock in the afternoon the following day. Making my way along the uneven pavement while carrying my earthly possessions in a big brown suitcase, I was walking down *Runcorn Road*. I checked the writing on the piece of paper in my rough hand. So this must be the address then I figured. I walked a few more steps, stopped then looked at the house with the number *29* written in thick chalk on it. The dirty nets in the front windows caught my eyes; the front door was dull and grotty. An old fat woman's face appeared at the front window, before it disappeared. With a bit of anxiety I knew this must be Stan's house. It did not impress me much from the outside, but with nowhere else to live, and letting out a heavy sigh I made my way up the path, through the weeds and overgrown grass, which I hasten to add nearly tripped me over as I went. I got to the front of the main door and knocked firmly onto it, there was no reply. I waited then knocked again. I was about to go back to the bus stop with the conclusion that this must be the incorrect address when I could hear shouting coming from inside.

Stan's voice was bellowing like a town crier from indoors. 'Are you going to open the door you silly old fat cow? You're sending me round the bloody twist woman.' I was cringing with embarrassment for I knew it was definitely Stan's dulcet tones all right. The front door slowly opened and Glad's powdered wrinkled face appeared with a pained expression. 'You must be Andrew,' she uttered in her cackling voice. 'Come in, come in. Me and Stan have been looking forward to your arrival.' The overwhelming scent of cheap lavender then came wafting in my direction from the old lady.

After entering the lounge I noticed Stan sitting in a dull green big armchair, puffing on his pipe, he sat up obviously happy to see me, 'Andrew, Andrew. It's good to see you, have a seat over there.' I put my heavy case down and slumped into the seat. Ah, I was relieved that at last the burden of my walking, plus numerous bus rides it had taken me to get to Stan's house was at an end.

Glad slowly waddled in. 'Would you like a nice cup of tea young man?' she cackled.

'That would be great, thanks.'

Glad waddled into the kitchen humming and singing. Looking around the room and thinking to myself with various notations I began observing the old lady - making a detailed assessment. My first *opinion* of Glad came as a bit of a surprise. She was an octogenarian plump lady. She was very much the opposite of Stan on the physical scale, him being slender in torso, and I reckon ten years her junior. Her obesity though, did not seem to hinder her movements that one would of concluded.

Stan let out a typical smoker's cough with his lungs obviously fighting the numerous amounts of chemicals sucked into them. 'What's on your mind Andy? Do you mind if I call you by that particular nickname?' he asked.

'No, not at all,' I joked.

'You will like it here,' he remarked with a slight smile in his ageing old face. 'Glad has done our spare room for you, and everything is in order.'

'Thanks Stan, I'm just thankful I'm away from my stepfather, and hopefully for good now. Perhaps I will be able to get some peace, without any bloody hassle.'

Stan bent over to a small dusty side table and picked up a notepad and pen, 'Right now for the rent.'

After I paid Stan some money his sister Glad entered with a pot of tea and a tray of cakes.

In the evening we had dinner and talked - with Stan and Glad in fine bantering form. But I was becoming tired as the hours passed and I readied an excuse before making my way to the spare room. I eventually got into the bed and decided to leave on the inadequate gas mantle, for I'd always been *nervous* of the dark. Mind you the damn lighting the mantle gave off was spooky enough. Tossing and turning trying to get some sleep I heard footsteps approaching:

'Who's there?' I shouted.

The bedroom door slowly creaked open, 'Stan... is that you?'

'No it's Glad,' she uttered in her distinct cackling voice. 'I've brought you a nice cup of drinking chocolate.'

I told Glad just to put it on the bedside table, she did as I requested, then waddled out closing the creaky white door. Picking up the drink I took a deep gulp. 'Oh Christ!' I fumed as my taste buds contracted. My face screwed up to *spit* this awful concoction of a drink out of my mouth. It had got salt in it instead of sugar. I retched a bit and *thought* that maybe Glad was senile or maybe half blind. Anyway I thought things can't get any worse, turning back into my bed I tried to settle down for a good night's sleep.

At three o clock in the morning everything seemed quiet, when abruptly I was woken by wailing singing, I can only describe it as sounding like an out of tune opera singer with piles. Grumbling and thinking who could be responsible for this awful noise I slowly opened and squinted my eyelids. The singing unfortunately continued to get louder. After looking at the clock by the side of my bed and noticing it was three-fifteen in the morning - this wailing singing continued to go on and off for the next two and a half hours. I tried to get back to sleep, but I could not, no matter how hard my body tried. How anybody was supposed to get any rest with this noise was beyond belief. I began 'cursing' and then could hear Stan shouting with some agitation.

'Shut up you stupid old fat cow!' I could hear him shout, obviously loud foul language followed up with strong effect. Suddenly banging sounds on the walls, and the muffled shouts of a raging man interrupted him: 'Shut up! People are trying to sleep round here!' It was coming from one of the unfortunate next-door neighbours. Stan still continued to carry on with his incessant screaming and shouting:

'Belt up Glad! You are sending everyone round the twist you silly old cow. You stupid—'

This time the male neighbour completely went off his tree with madness and roared, 'I'll Commit Murder! I Will Commit Murder.'

A woman's scream, high in pitch could be heard pleading, 'No…Jack don't, he's mad. No!'

I put my head under my pillow tightly to block out this torment. Stan for some reason next took it upon himself to whistle loudly, which continued for the next forty minutes, this caused the neighbour's patience to finally snap and he roared his complete disapproval. 'I CAN'T STAND THIS!'

The massive smash of an object shook against the wall of Stan's house. It must have been of some tremendous weight for it made the whole place shake in its foundations.

My thoughts were irrational and went into overdrive at this commotion, 'What have I done? I'm living with a bunch of raving nutcases.' I groaned a little, before I let out some more words:

'What have I let myself in for?' I yawned which contorted my face due to tiredness. I was so sleep weary that I felt a momentary sickness, I tiredly closed my eyes for relief of what little sleep I could now manage to get, and prayed for the noise to die down.

At breakfast time I did not say much. Glad and Stan were sitting down at the table and eating their breakfast with numerous slurping noises and the odd feature of breaking wind. I noticed Glad's false teeth fought to digest her food; they seemed to have a mind of their own.

Stan dipped a piece of bread into his egg and uttered a few words to me, 'Good night's sleep Andy?'

I reacted with irritation. 'You're joking Stan. What was all that commotion about in the early morning?'

Stan seemed a bit apologetic in his manner and reply. 'I'm sorry about that. It's Glad. She does like to burst into song in the early hours. I'm afraid you're just going to have to get used to it.' He then turned to Glad and spoke a few words with his usual wit.

'I told you he would like it here.'

Glad poured some tea for Stan and myself while mumbling, 'Yes *bruv* I know.'

A sense of bewilderment enveloped me due to their strange communications.

Stan then looked thoughtful and told me: 'There's everything in the whites of an egg that a man's carcass requires. Elegancy is sufficiency...And before you study the works of Karl Marx. Read The Four Values Of Capitalism.'

I was confused by his sentence - but just countered with the phrase: 'Whatever you say Stan, it's your viewpoint.'

Unfortunately Glad had to let out her awful cackling laugh at my expense, with a short burst of breaking wind which was beginning to offend me. She asked 'whether I had anything planned for today.' I said to her that 'I would try asking around the town to see what jobs were going about locally.' I needed some money to sustain me, seeing that my army pay was just about exhausted.

Stan spoke to me with optimism as I was getting up from the breakfast table, the blue patterned cloth covering it decorated with egg stains. 'You will find something. There are always jobs going around this way...Many a more, or many a day as my local priest used to say to his big old dog as it squatted down to shit.' I laughed in stunned amusement at his comments and prepared to quickly be on my way to find work.

Chapter 3

After Death Suggestions

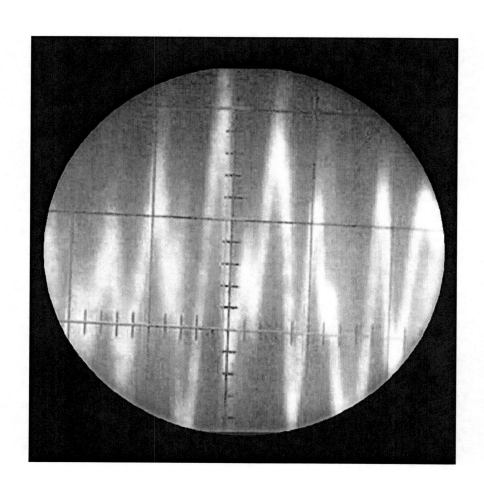

About eight months had now gone by. I myself had managed to gain some kind of employment as a warehouse driver. But gradually the toil of living with Stan and Glad was beginning to affect my nerves, I never felt comfortable bringing a lady back as I could never get the two old characters to go out together. I needed my own space, so I was looking around for a home of my own. I needed to escape to a place of solitude, and have my privacy returned. I did not tell Stan and Glad of my intentions until I'd signed a tenancy agreement for a place, and possibly one night I would sneak off and disappear from their company.

One early evening, I was sitting down in the murky living room around the grubby fireplace, the flames burning and giving a feeling of warmth. Glad sat upright on the green chair to the opposite of me, and Stan was fiddling about the room as usual.

'Work treating you well? It's been about seven months now,' said the old man as he tried to adjust the worn out gas mantle light.

'Yes it's fine Stan,' I replied while looking around at the poor lighting in the room. I had *told* Stan on numerous occasions that he had to get the electricity sorted out for his house, before he burnt the blasted place down. The gas was making it completely unsafe, and the lighting, well if you could call it lighting, what with the smoke from the open fire, the coal ash, plus Glad and Stan's smoking - it was like living in a pollution ridden smog. Stan then spoke with his usual ignorance of the facts, 'Naa it does me and my sister fine. That's the way it's been, and that's the way I want it.' He lit up his big long pipe and continued, 'Anyway Andy. I've got to ask you something, did you learn a trade while you were doing your service in the army?'

'Not really,' I remarked with an edge of deference. 'I was in the infantry. All you learn to do in there is to kill in a gruesome number of ways, as many of your enemies as possible. Plus the endless cleaning and picking up of rubbish. Then getting a punch in the face from the sergeant or your corporal if he was having a bad day. More often or not they would do this if they had not managed to get their leg over with the local tarts from the town where you were stationed.'

Stan turned to Glad and told her to get a couple of cans of ale for him and myself. Next Stan blew out puffs of smoke from his pipe in my direction and informed me 'that while he was in the army in about 1921, he'd decided to take up the distinguished art of medicine, accompanied with relevant surgery.'

I did not believe him and teased him in a sarcastic reply, 'Oh come off it. You don't give off a feeling, attaining to be medically competent to me in that area.'

Stan assured me and pointed to a certificate of surgical procedures in first aid, hanging on the smoke stained lounge wall. I got up and examined it thinking it must be a forgery, but by my own judgment it seemed to be genuine.

'I've always fancied myself as a fellow of the London Hospital elite,' he commented.

As I sat back down, Stan also told me that he'd performed a minor operation on Glad, with the aid of a small screwdriver ground down to a knife edge, some matchsticks to act as probes, cotton wall, antiseptic and a pair of tweezers. This procedure helped remove a small lump from Glad's large thigh. I was a little surprised, but it must have worked seeing Glad was still alive, and did not lose her leg in the process. 'I never knew,' I said: 'You are a man of numerous hidden talents.'

Stan replied back to me in his usual manner. 'It's nice to know that I've managed to achieve something worthwhile, other than my drinking exploits. Seeing I am in the winter of my years.' He pulled out his handkerchief and blew his nose loudly. Glad seemed to be quite *tired* by now, she bid us both 'goodnight' and retired to her bed upstairs. There was then a mellow silence for a couple of minutes; Stan seemed to be in a reflective mood. For some reason, he decided to poke me in the arm for a response, 'Andrew, I'm glad she has gone up to bed. I have something I want to discuss with you.'

'What's troubling you?' I replied. I was then interrupted by some homely comforts. The first fall of winter rain announced its arrival by hitting hard on the window overlooking the garden, and the old clock chimed in its out of tune sound accompanied by the sizzle of wood burning on the fire.

'Seriously,' asked Stan with emotion in his voice. 'What do you think becomes of us...Beyond the grave?'

'That's a strange question coming from you.' I began chuckling at his words. 'There's nothing, when you are dead that's it. No angels, no harps, no bloody living up in the clouds with religious music. That's it!'

Stan protested. 'Andy, boy - I need to know there is something. There has to be.'

I thought to myself that Stan was a confirmed atheist; I never thought he'd been very religious or anything supernatural like that. I had never believed in anything religious. Many a time I used to row with the army chaplain, who used to say quite categorically, 'it is fine to kill' and other ridiculous notions. This intensified my own dismissive viewpoint about the subject.

Stan came out with another strange quote. 'I believe in ghosts,' he said sternly. 'Cause I have seen one.'

'Don't be ridiculous. There is no such thing.'

'It's true Andy, seriously you must believe me.'

'Alright, so you did see a ghost, what exactly are you getting at Stan?' I said.

Stan looked at me with a solemn expression and asked me a third serious question. 'Now Andy, whoever of us was to die, and break free from his mortal coil first, would find a way somehow, to let the other one know that they have survived, and would make a *sign* indicating there is a spirit world, or afterlife beyond this life of grief and tears.'

I must admit I'd no idea that Stan was so pessimistic about his current existence, so I was obnoxious in my reply to him:

'Don't talk daft Stan, even the psychic debunker *Houdini* promised somehow he would let people know he had survived death, especially to his beloved wife *Bess*. But there is no evidence that he has been able to make any kind of sign to confirm this, from what I have read in books.'

'That may be the case,' Stan questioned in a glum manner. 'But I mean what I said before.' There was a thoughtful pause - then a *phrase* came like a biblical quote from his beer-moistened lips.

'"Time is the essence. For the rest of my Duties". These will be the words I will use to tell you it is really me who has made contact with you after my death.' He became more emotional as he repeated it again. '*Time is the essence. For the rest of my Duties,* remember Andy.' I was feeling skeptical, but in the end I agreed. He also made me promise him, that if he were to die first, I would look after financial matters and Glad's welfare, as she was becoming frailer now. He looked with a wistful expression at the picture of young Glad next to himself on the ornate mantelpiece. I was a little hesitant, but I *promised* him that I would carry out his wishes.

The coal fire, mixed with wood burning in the old dirty fireplace started to die down, and I looked at the clock - the evening had flown by. As I got up deciding to make my way to bed I told Stan that I was going to be away for a couple of weeks, I was enrolling to go on a course, which was happening in Maidstone and that I'd be staying with an old friend - Michael from my army days.

'Two weeks,' said Stan shocked.

'It's only fourteen days,' I said as I stepped out the door. 'I will be going very early in the morning. Hopefully I will miss the delights of Glad's opera crescendo.'

Stan guffawed while telling me *not to work to hard.* 'Have a good time Andy boy, I will wish you luck. Also, will you be trying to get your leg over with some fat woman or trollop?'

'I beg your pardon!'

Stan let out a wild laugh.

I was not seeing his sense of humour after talking about *death* for most of the evening, however I quipped back. 'Don't worry Stan, I intend to.' Then I bid him goodnight before retiring to my bed.

It was four o clock, the following morning, and I quietly shut the front door to the house and made my way up the overgrown path carrying my case. I turned behind me briefly and I could hear Glad was bursting into song again. Stan started screaming and shouting and the neighbour's lights came on in a domino fashion. I quickened my step eager to get away from the house. I chuckled to myself and thought with amusement. They were definitely a right pair; they have got over the top eccentric, bordering on the compulsive personalities. Mind you, I paused for a moment as their screaming and shouting was breaking the pleasant sound of early morning birdsong. I can't accuse them of senile dementia. On the contrary, both are too colourful and on the ball, when it comes down to the material needs for surviving and paying their way. I wish I'd not made that 'stupid promise' I gave to Stan agreeing that I'd take care of Glad if any mishap or illness befell him. But I suppose after a few weeks with a bit of luck he will have forgotten about it, as he trudges round the numerous ale house he often frequented.

Chapter 4

Stan Meets His Enemy

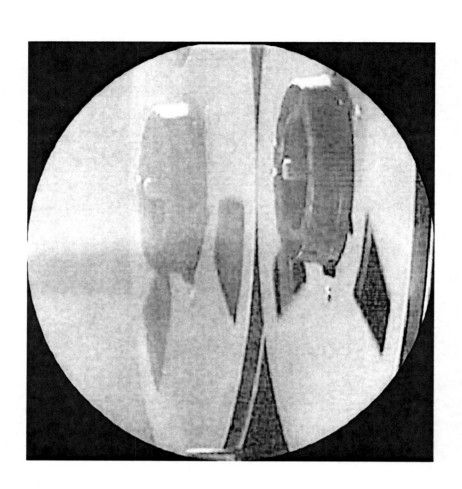

The *Flag and Dog* pub began emptying of its usual colourful characters. Eleven o clock in the evening meant last orders were sounded. Stan was his typical drunken self as he set out on the routine journey to take him back home. Loud singing was heard in the background and a fellow customer told Stan to take it easy as he'd had a skinful that evening.

'Don't worry, I will be fine,' he replied in a slurred tone. Stan then 'belched' loudly. Further on, when he was walking down a dimly lit street staggering and laughing he began talking to himself, 'Oh what a night. Oh what a wonderful night.'

He passed a narrow dark alley with not much consideration. But waiting in the alley was Ted the Barman, the man from the pub that Stan had spat on a few months earlier. Ted the Barman walked out of the alley, his metal toecap shoes making scraping and grinding sounds. Then a dog's ugly howl caused sinister echoes and a few dustbins fell over in the distance. There was an eerie wind - and Ted scratched his unshaven face while eyeing Stan up and down with a menacing glare. He began grinning like the devil himself.

'Now I am going to give him something to remember me by.' He began to follow Stan with a quickness of his step. Stan thought he could hear footsteps behind him. He stopped and turned around nervously, 'Anyone there?' he shouted, 'Arthur is that you?' Stan *stared* hard into darkness but could see nothing; he turned back around and carried on with his journey.

The Barman started walking faster, gritting his yellow chipped teeth while rubbing his sweaty clenched fist with a metal knuckle-duster wrapped around it. Stan could hear the footsteps getting closer and he was overcome with dread, he knew he had to try and run. In a fearful tone he blurted out:

'Leave me alone!'

Stan detoured to a short cut over a demolition area, and nearly stumbled over some rubble. Turning to stare behind him he shouted, 'Get away from me!' By this time the Barman had sneaked in front of Stan and now stood only a few feet directly parallel to him. Stan quickly moved his head to an opposite position. Then suddenly, and with a facade of horror - Stan came face to face with Ted the Barman - who was growling with fury. Instantly, Stan's shirt was grabbed and Ted uttered in a malicious voice, 'I've been really looking forward to this moment.' He pushed his forearm up to Stan's and punched the old man hard in his right eye with his fist. Stan screamed in pain due to the force of the blow, made even more powerful with the knuckle-duster Ted was wearing. Stan put both his hands up and hung on with desperation, he gripped onto Ted's hair, they both struggled, and there were violent kicks viciously catching Stan on his legs.

'Leave me alone,' begged Stan, 'help me! Please!' Abruptly his shirt was ripped during the struggle, and the pushing and violence of the attack made Stan's wallet fall out of his back trouser pocket. Ted was becoming more aggressive - he seemed to enjoy his humiliating threatening behaviour. In a hoarse angry voice he snarled, 'How do you feel now old man?' He laughed and punched Stan hard in the stomach, which sent the unfortunate elderly victim plunging backwards. Stan staggered and fell over some concrete rubble, hitting the rocky dusty ground with a thump. A couple of peoples' voices in the distance seemed to be coming nearer and Ted was disturbed that he might be seen, at that moment he started running away but still uttered a few words in Stan's direction:

'I enjoyed that, I hope that will put you in your own grave for certain now.' Then he made his escape by disappearing into the shadows of the moonlit night.

Stan was groaning and doubled up in agony, he let out a few moaning words in between coughs and heavy breaths to try and aid him with his distress. 'Oh my legs, my stomach is in pain.' Stan touched his face with a bloodstained hand and let out a sickening cough, luckily for him near the road he could hear a man and woman 'chatting.' He shouted for 'assistance.' The couple walking nearby heard Stan's groans and went to his aid. The man ran over and gazed down with a shocked expression:

'Mate are you alright?' he asked. The man shouted to his girlfriend, 'Christ Shelia! He looks like he has taken a right hammering.'

Stan tried to get up; his face now besieged in agony. 'Please help me. Please!' He asked in torrid discomfort. 'I've been attacked, can you try and help me get home.' He fought the pain to make his injured chest become able to take a breath of night air. The man and woman helped Stan up gently, he gave them directions and the three of them struggled back to Stan's house. They managed to get to the entrance of his house. Glad *heard* a loud knock on the main door; she made her way with difficulty out of her bed and went downstairs. Glad adjusted the hall gas mantle for some light before she slowly opened the heavy front door. She saw *Stan* being supported by the couple. He was breathing heavily, with blood dripping from his face. Glad let out a hysterical scream:

'*STANNNNNNNN!*'

I'd been away for two weeks on my course in Maidstone, and it had been a hectic time. Nevertheless, and after many inquires, all accompanied with the reading of many newspaper advertisements - I'd finally found a flat for myself. I was going to break the news to Stan and Glad that 'I would be leaving their company soon.'

It was a sunny afternoon and I arrived at the house and knocked on the old front door. Strange I thought, I would normally hear Stan shouting and hollering at Glad, this would be the usual occurrence. I knocked again and waited, Glad opened the door slowly and seemed detached of her normal graceful mannerism, well that was my conclusion.

'Andy,' she said with a relieved expression. 'Oh dear...please come in.'

I asked cordially, 'how she was.' Glad's face seemed pale and drawn. 'What's the matter?' I commented as I stepped into the lounge. She shut the front door and followed me with a slight limp in her walk. Glad then sat down and let out a heavy sigh.

'Where is Stan?' I said flippantly. 'Don't tell me he is down the pub boozing it up again.' Glad shook her head slowly and told me Stan lay upstairs in his bed. I asked her 'what was he doing in bed at this time.' She pulled out a tissue; her hands were shaking, and she blew her nose while wiping her bloodshot eyes. 'Stan had an accident the night after you left, falling over some uneven pavement slabs he told me. But I believe he was beaten up. Go upstairs and have *er butchers* for yourself. I have had terrible trouble with him. The doctor has been called out to try to assist him, but Stan reckons he knows far more than the doctor and told him to get lost. I worry so much. Oh dear he can be so stubborn sometimes. I don't know what to do.'

I told Glad that I would see if I could get any sense out of the old fool as she looked shattered. Glad told me he'd made her go back and forth to the local chemist to get him all matter of potions, this had made her feel so tired, also causing her hip to become more painful with all the exertion of doing Stan's ridiculous errands. She let out a heavy breath and rubbed her ankle. We talked a bit more before I made my way upstairs to speak to him. I approached Stan's bedroom entrance and waited for a moment, then I slowly pushed open the door. The strawberry coloured curtains were half drawn, and there were numerous plates, cups, medicine bottles and pills, scattered around the room, softly I said:

'Stan are you awake?'

He grunted as he strained to sit up in bed. I helped him as best I could - trying to avoid the various objects on the floor.

He coughed and sounded groggy: 'I've been in the wars, I suppose you can say. You would not believe how much my face has swollen up and how tender my stomach is now.' I approached him for a closer examination and he looked dreadful, his right eye was swollen up immensely, while the rest of his face was purple and black, plus his right arm was in a plaster cast. Eyeing him up and down I angrily demanded, 'Who has done this violence towards you?'

Stan with some hesitation articulated to me that he'd fallen over some object on the pavement and banged his head on the roadside kerb after leaving a pub, caused by too much drink.

In a snappy tone I said, 'Come on Stan! Someone has giving you a right hiding, you can't kid me.'

He gazed straight at me. 'Maybe you are right. It's my own fault. I've made quite a few enemies round here. But what is done is done...I'm the one lying here in this bed.'

A few moments later he pulled up his nightshirt. 'Here, press your fist into my chest.'

I declined his offer, not wanting to inflict added damage to his battered body. Nevertheless, Stan insisted this crazed action be performed on him. As he thought for some peculiar reason - if you kept *pushing* around a damaged chest it would get better by reducing the swelling, this was the ludicrous state of his medical knowledge that 'I dismissed with utter contempt.' Then he wanted me to go to the chemist and get him a diathermy protractor. What an earth it was God only knows. I subsequently tried to reason some sense into him: 'Look,' I said, 'let me go and get the doctor, he can help you better than anyone else, besides Glad is worried sick about you.'

Stan was becoming angry and shouted his disapproval. 'No! I can treat myself thank you. I do not need some bloody idiot to start poking and examining me again. I know more about medicine than he will ever know.'

I shook my head with despair and told him that he was a right stuck up stubborn bastard. 'Stan as far as I'm concerned I will let you get on with it, you stupid ignorant fool.' I turned away and stormed out of the bedroom, slamming the door behind me. Stan then started shouting insults:

'Yeah that's right. You can piss off with the damn doctor and all the other do *gooders*. The lot of you stink, do you hear…stink!' He picked up a medicine bottle and threw it with all his energy at the bedroom door causing the bottle to shatter into many pieces.

Over the next few days Stan's health started to deteriorate rapidly, plus there were indications his mental state was also becoming pretty flaky. I desperately wanted to move out and into my new flat, but my 'bloody promise' I made to Stan meant I had to at least look after his sister Glad, well until he got better. But it was while me and Glad was sitting down to breakfast one morning that we began to hear the strange sound of Stan starting to 'recite' the *Lord's Prayer*. This surprised me. I thought in my opinion he was a confirmed atheist when it came to religious matters.

Stan then began banging on the ceiling, shouting for me to come upstairs with the words that there was a giant snake crawling up his bedroom wall. I dropped my teacup on the table and made my way to his bedroom to see him. When I entered his room Stan was waving his arms about and throwing things at the wall.

'Stan what's wrong?' I asked in a startled manner.

Stan kept going on about a snake, a massive one, moving all around the walls. Then he uttered: 'There's spiders! Giant spiders here Andy! Please help me? Grab my cane to beat them away into the drains.'

I looked closely around but could see nothing. Stan was still raving so I thought it best to do what he wanted. I ran over to his wardrobe, which was in the corner and took hold of Stan's big Victorian walking cane. I bashed it up the walls and the ceiling to fend of these hallucinations - Stan was continually shouting words with fear. Medicine bottles and other items fell over under my clumsy footsteps; some breaking due to all the action, but after a few minutes I'd managed to chase off these imaginary snakes with their spider counterparts.

Glad was panicking downstairs and was shrieking:

'What is going on up there Andrew?' She repeated my name again even louder. 'Andrew!!!'

'For Christ sake,' I yelled with agitation. 'Shut up Glad please. I am trying to deal with the situation.' I put the wooden cane on the floor and walked over to Stan, his eyes were squinted and closed with his body shaking in fear. I tried to be reassuring in my comments, 'There is nothing there anymore, and I've chased all the snakes and spiders from your room, see for yourself.' I pointed this fact out to him. Stan slowly opened his glazed eyes - and looked around in a periscope mode. He then struggled to sit up to a higher position in his bed; I helped him as best I could. Stan was *adamant* that he could 'not hold on much longer.'

I was dismissive with my reply back to him, 'No you are not Stan.' Telling me that he thought he was going to die had incensed me.

'Andy,' the old man uttered with a crack in his voice.

I interrupted. 'Listen *fella* come on. Glad needs you. What do you think will happen to her if you die.' I hoped in my mind that my phrase had been compassionate. I then put my clean shaven face close up to his eyes and told him that 'her spirit would be broken if anything happened.' Stan rubbed his chest and said, 'I will try Andy, why did I have to end up like this. Why?'

'Because you have refused to see the doctor. You won't go to the hospital, and I can't do anymore. Do you understand me!'

'I'm sorry for being a pain in the arse,' voiced Stan with a mellow response. We talked a little longer and I stayed with him for a further twenty minutes until he drifted off into a light sleep. I quietly shut the bedroom door and tiptoed downstairs to where Glad was sitting.

'Stan has calmed down now, I've talked some sense into him and he is now asleep,' I said.

Glad thanked me for my help, which brought a relieved composure to her haggard face, 'I just hope he can pull through this terrible time Andrew,' she replied. I turned to Glad and told her I was off to work and if Stan got worse to call the doctor's telephone number from the phone box, no matter how much he argued not to. I also gave her my work telephone number and told her to call me if things were getting really serious. We said goodbye and I made my way off to work. The events with Stan over the last few days were causing unwanted pressure to take their toll on my nerves. I knew that I needed a good few drinks round the local pub later in the evening to help me with the stress, liven up my mood, and also to remove this pit in the stomach sensation, which now afflicted me.

Chapter Five

Visions of the Light

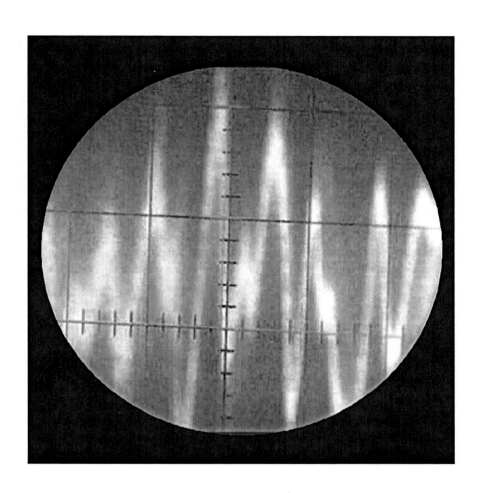

It was now ten thirty in the evening. I had been having some drinks with my work friends, and I was quite cheerful. Thomas and his wife were standing outside the pub with me, sixties style music played loudly from within the bar accompanied with happy singing, which brought an atmosphere of calm to refresh my weary mind.

Thomas put his hand on my shoulder and asked, 'Hey Andrew, stay the night with me and my wife this evening. Take it from a friend - you need to get away from that old couple you are shacked up with, they would send me mad. Come on Andrew what do you say?'

I pondered for a moment and shook my head: 'Thanks for the offer Thom, but Stan is very ill at the moment and I can't leave Glad with him too long, in case he plays up again.' I then studied my gold plated wristwatch and I knew I had better get back to check on them as it was getting late. Thomas put his arm around the waist of his wife and we said our goodbyes:

'I will see you tomorrow Andy,' Thomas joked.

I nodded and then began to walk back too Stan's and Glad's abode. A few steps into my journey a *man* bumped rudely into my shoulder, I stopped and asked this person for an apology. He spun round and eyed me up and down. The man happened to be Ted the Barman. I recognized him immediately.

'How's your old man friend. Is he suffering with pain?' he said without pity. I stood still for a second and was tempted to punch him in the face, but I did not have the time, or feel in the mood for fighting this night, especially with this burly lump of humanity. So I did not acknowledge his question and carried on with my journey to avoid trouble. The thought though now preyed on my mind, could this be Stan's mystery attacker, I would ask the old man when I saw him in a few minutes.

Meanwhile, back at the house Glad was in the kitchen cleaning up. Stan then banged on the ceiling asking for her to come upstairs to tend to him, Glad groaned as her back ached, also the rest of her limbs had become extremely painful with all the errands and help she was giving to Stan. She slowly clambered up the stairs, pushed open the bedroom door and asked him 'what was wrong.' The old man was mumbling to himself and saying he had never felt so ill and so tired. He let out a heaving cough while instructing Glad to turn him over onto his side as his whole body ached because of lying in the same position for most of the day. She helped him to turn over, feeling the strain as she did this: remember she was over eighty years of age. Glad asked Stan 'if he wanted anything to drink.' But he told her his lemonade, would suffice his thirst for the moment.

'I just need to rest,' he said.

Glad tidied his room as best she could and after that she made her way out of the bedroom and back downstairs. Stan's pale thin face stared wearily at the clock on his side table in the dimly lit bedroom as he drifted in and out of consciousness; he slowly began to struggle for breath and his breathing became heavier. Stan even with his obscure medical knowledge *knew* that he was about to die. Fear overcame him and he tried letting out a few words, 'I'm sorry…I'm so remorseful for what I've…done in my life. Please God I don't want to die like—' Suddenly at that moment Stan clutched his chest, moaned in pain, his eyes began to close and at that moment he died. He then experienced a death *vision*. At that moment he had a mental picture of himself and Glad as children holding hands, and walking through a beautiful garden, smelling the fresh beautiful air. The scent of the flowers, and a wonderful sunshine lit the whole landscape; it had a dreamy feel to it. A minute or so later Glad stopped and took a step backward.

'Sister, why have you stopped?' asked Stan.

She immediately waved goodbye and continued to walk in another direction.

'Glad! Glad don't go!' he begged.

His words were no use as Glad carried on into the yellow coloured horizon. Stan felt alone and hurriedly ran after his sister shouting her 'name' but she vanished.

Suddenly the atmosphere changed, it began to darken and become oppressive. Stan looked nervously around, two fierce aggressive wolf like type dogs were running in his direction, there was then explosions in the sky and to his horror he saw a head in the ground pop up in front of him. Stan stopped in shock while observing it. The head began to change into an apparition - solidifying fleshy tones gradually formed into the features of 'Ted the Barman', the man who had beaten him up from the pub and had contributed to his untimely death. The head with the body began to *rise* up from the ground in front of Stan, it was carrying a hefty club, and its 'face' was contorted in 'anger and hate.' Stan turned and ran screaming. Next strange blackbirds bigger than crows swooped in the awe inspiring orange sky - enlightening behind the apparition of Ted. Ted then moved closer to the old man - before letting out a hideous laugh.

Stan stumbled and fell onto the grassy ground, but instead of landing normally like he expected would happen, he passed through the surface as if it was butter. He then began to fall downwards while spinning fast, it was dark and voices and cries were heard all around him.

'Help me!' he cried, 'Glad, Andy please!' Then he felt a whirling sensation pulling him into a glorious white light. A window mysteriously opened up in the darkness and Stan could see his sister walking up the stairs towards the bedroom:

'Glad!' he screamed with his arms outstretched to try to touch her. 'I'm alive! Here can you see meeeeeeee?'

Glad entered the bedroom and was shocked to see Stan's lifeless body lying on the bed, she *touched* it but it was cold. She then let out an hysterical scream: 'No Stan don't die. I need you!' There was a blistering flash, an explosive bang and Stan was sucked into the bright light of infinity, away from this world and into the next, whatever that should be. Glad then put her head in her wrinkly hands and started sobbing loudly.

I was just approaching the outside of Stan's house, when a flash of orange sparks hit me, I shivered and for some unexplained reason felt an invisible hand strike out at my face, causing a loud slap noise to be clearly heard in my left ear. A blue *mist* appeared just a few feet in front of me, and then with a flash it was gone. I jolted and felt immensely cold all over. I *knew* at that very moment that Stan was *Dead*. I cannot explain how I knew this, but I just sensed this. Let us say it had that experience you sometimes get when someone is about to call you, you guess who it will be but you cannot explain it. Or of bad news that was coming through the post, maybe though I was a bit psychic. I ran the few more yards to Stan's house and could see Glad standing distraught outside. I stopped, we looked at each other, and then she began to break down sobbing. I realised now that Stan must be definitely dead.

After a couple of hours I informed the doctor of the situation as we were going to need a 'death certificate' for the burial. Little did I know that Stan had no insurance to cover his own demise, which was typical. Only after a week of letters and pleading phone calls made by myself did the local council finally reluctantly intervene and arranged for a burial to take place.

On a Thursday, nearly a week and a half after Stan's death I attended his funeral. Glad and a friend of hers were the only other mourners in attendance. It was a dull miserable day with the rain hitting hard on the small chapel roof; it was eleven thirty in the morning. I looked solemnly at the casket and then at Glad who was quiet and drawn, her friend giving her support as best she could. The vicar opened his prayer book and lifted up his head from a bowed position.

'May we sing the hymn "Death is no End",' he said. I listened but did not sing though; Glad sang some of the words with sorrow in her voice. After the brief service Glad, her friend and myself went outside following the light brown wooden coffin. It was lifted by the pallbearers out of the chapel and taken towards a deep paupers' grave, the rest of us were walking slowly behind it until we arrived at the spot of burial. The coffin was lowered without much dignity alongside the other coffins stacked up in the burial hole.

The vicar opened his bible, and with a solemn tone spoke a passage: 'Though I walk through the shadow of death. I will feel no evil. Believe in God. For he is the life and is the resurrection.'

During the vicar's sermon my mind began thinking about many things. So this was how poor old Stan ends up. After all his life and adventures. The eccentric old man may have had pessimistic views of any thing religious, but he did have some hope that there might be 'something' after the cessation of physical life. What with his belief in ghosts and other spiritual matters, there has got to be something after this, or has there? I dug into my pocket and pulled out a scrap piece of paper. On it, it had the line *Time Is The Essence. For The Rest Of My Duties* scrawled in ink.

I stared hard at the words remembering this was the 'phrase' that Stan would use to indicate he had survived beyond the boundaries of death. I put the piece of paper back into my damp side trouser pocket and gave one more glimpse back at the grave. The vicar finished his address and this was now the signal for the gravediggers to start their morbid work of shovelling the damp earth into the grave. Myself, and Glad who had her friend for comfort walked slowly away towards a waiting car, Glad was still sobbing. The two gravediggers I noticed were sniggering as they were doing their job. I heard a few of their nasty jokes they were saying about the recently buried coffins, I looked at them with disgust. One of the gravediggers was laughing and basically mocking the dead. His glazed eyes then caught mine, 'Is *there* a problem boy?'

'No not really,' I replied. I carried on a few more steps before turning around and telling them, 'You think it's funny to laugh do you? Well just remember you will end up in a hole one day. No one is *immortal* my friend.' I turned back towards the direction of the chapel where I quickened my step so I could catch up with the distraught Glad who was holding her friend's hand.

Things did get worse over the next few months for Glad, tragedy was still to follow, for she had a fall while doing some cleaning in her dimly gas mantled lit house while I'd been away at work, and the old lady died a few days later of pneumonia complications. I think she lost the desire to live after her brother had died. So at last my *promise* to Stan to look after her had been kept and I was now free of its terms. I would now be back in the wild open world, preparing for life's next adventure. Little did I know that in twenty-years time the name 'Stan' and the proof for 'life after death' would re-enter my life, with unknown consequences.

Part 2

The Year 1985

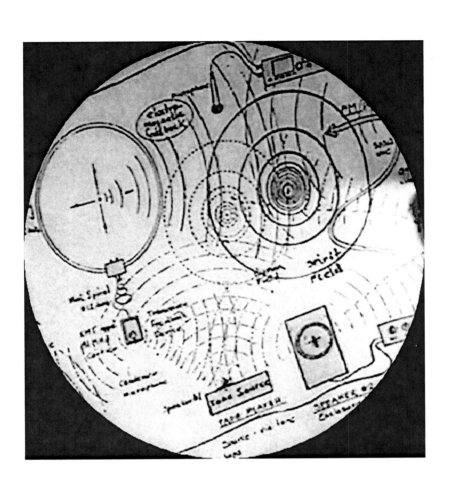

Well I made my way through the years and decades of the 1960s, 1970s, and to my present point of time 1985. My life went through many phases; I suppose this is part of the learning process, which for some unknown reason defines our course of existence. After the death of Stan, and later on Glad, I moved on, with my Army career finished I did find the concept of the civilian way of life's work a puzzle. I left my job as the warehouse driver and moved up to Newcastle to find out what I might try my hand at next. Of course there were drugs which I experimented with, it's fashion endemic of those days. But I found the concept of smoking grass, experimenting with magic mushrooms, doing barbiturates, and inevitably LSD an unsatisfying distraction. What was the point, if I wanted to get out of my face then a bottle of *Jack Daniels* whisky would suffice, at least it wasn't illegal. At the end of the 1960s, I still seemed no nearer in deciding in what I wanted to do.

So I came back from Newcastle and returned to Maidstone towards the beginning of the 1970s, a year of outlandish fashion, the three-day week due to the numerous strikes, which seemed a way of life at the time, and novelty fads. After a brief courtship I met and married my first wife Jacqueline in 1974, we met through friends and at first everything seemed fine. Problems started though, I myself did not want any children, the reason for this being the experience of going through a particularly unpleasant childhood. For me this was reinforced and exacerbated by the death of my real father in Korea, his place then taken by a thuggish stepfather. My selfish attitude on this and other matters caused my marriage to Jacqueline to fracture. We stayed together for only two years overall before the divorce became set in stone. The *financial* repercussions of this escapade cost me a lot of money with my ex-wife obtaining half of everything I possessed, including me losing the house. I'd no time to mope around though and swiftly got myself together.

Nevertheless, during my time with Jacqueline the subject of electronics had entered into me life and became an unusual hobby for me to lose time in. So with that in mind, I decided to go to college to learn this skill in depth to improve my career prospects. After a few years I gained the relevant qualifications and got a well-paid job in this field. Subsequently came the beginning of the 1980s, and my second marriage to Anna, everything now seemed *perfect* in my life.

For some reason however - I became attracted to Spiritualism and the Paranormal. I must admit I had never before been interested in this subject. Although it stayed in the back of my mind, for in early 1982, my mother died. This event affected me like it would for any other grieving relative. I did feel numb and weepy even during the funeral and for months afterwards, but eventually I managed to free myself from the grief and return to my normal way of life.

One night, after looking through some of my old documents, searching for the legal papers regarding my mother's estate and her 'Last Will and Testament', I found a scrap of brown paper in a plastic sleeve. The words written on it were:

Time Is The Essence. For The Rest Of My Duties.

These were the actual words the old man Stan made me write down before his own death, they were supposed to indicate if ever one day *he* made communication in some form or another, this sentence would prove him, and only him had made contact. Maybe due to this and the death of my mother I decided to consult a couple of Spiritualist Mediums. I wondered if any genuine information would be forthcoming, unfortunately this proved pointless as the responses and answers to my questions from the 'Psychic Mediums' were vague and wrong, this caused an abrupt end to my interest in the paranormal field for now.

In early 1984, Anna and me moved to a nice semi-detached house in the small village of Oakley in Herefordshire. Due to Anna's requests, we acquired a couple of pets, a boxer dog by the name of Rex, and one cat called Tiger.

Over my work years I had managed to amass a wide selection of electronic equipment, mainly due to my job I was doing for the electronic company. Everything seemed to be turning out fine; my hopes and confidences were premature indeed. This would now be a good point to continue the second instalment of my story.

LET PART 2 OF THE STORY BEGIN!

Electronic Ghosts appearing on the Television screen.

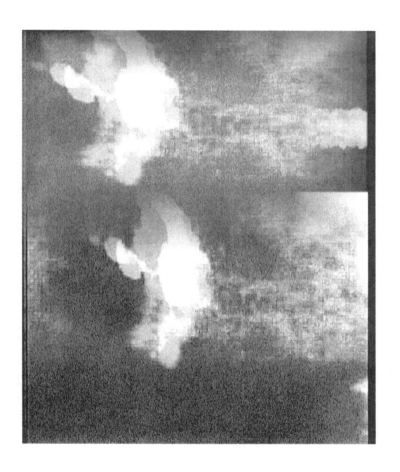

Chapter 6

Unemployment

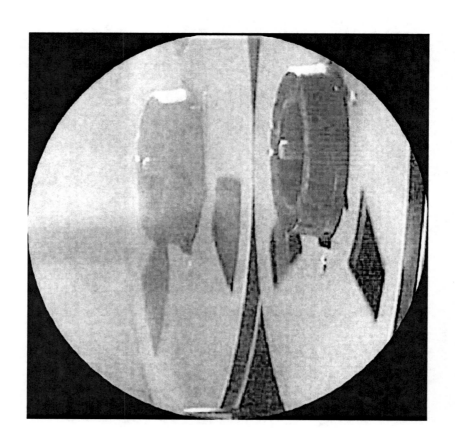

1985

My age had unfortunately accumulated another twenty years, making me forty-two with the many ailments which affected me. I now lived in the height of yuppies and wealth that were the symptoms of the progressive Thatcher Revolution. The year was 1985. I myself had worked as an electronic engineer for about three years now. The video and entertainment industry had really taken off and I'd gained quite a bit of expertise in this sort of repair, and the building of some of these commercial devices. But I'm afraid my fortune was about to change, Mr. Bains, my boss, called me up into his office to break some devastating news. In his office his manner seemed brash and very abrupt. He turned around from looking through the large window to break the news.

'I am going to have to let you go from the company,' he commented. Mr. Bains gave me a letter of *termination* of my employment.

I glanced through it shocked. 'You mean after all these years you are going to sack me!' Mr. Bains told me that the company was transferring most of its operations to the Far East. The simple facts meant that poorer, but more experienced people were breaking the mould in this field of electronics – they were in abundance, and inhabited that region to the full. Also they worked very hard for peanuts: fellow colleagues and myself could never achieve this absurd work ethic in our own country.

I slammed my fist hard on his desk and angrily dismissed his reasons. 'Don't give me that!' I exclaimed. 'I will tell you what the real reason is. Never mind the qualifications or how loyal you have been. The workforce over there is dirt cheap and you can pay them a pittance.'

My boss backed off away from me while trying to give more stupid answers to my questions. 'Go away Andrew! You are no longer part of this company anymore.'

I came back with a frustrated and angry answer. 'Bullshit! Money that's all it has come down to in Thatcher's Britain, bloody money do you hear me?' Mr. Bains put his hand out in some kind of gesture towards me, to try and make matters calm down, but the writing had been written in the sand, I knew that I would be losing my highly paid job. I now was a member of an exclusive sorry club - I would be joining the other three million people languishing on the dole. Before I left Mr. Bains' office I kicked over one of his highly modern new chairs and slammed the door extremely hard.

Outside in the town an hour later I was walking aimlessly around feeling terrible guilt. I stepped out in the road and got nearly hit by a car. I jumped while holding up my hands in apology. The car driver leaned out of his automobile side window clenching his fist abusively, 'You stupid arsehole! Watch where you are going.' His car sped off making a screeching sound due to the wheels spinning on the damp road.

I gave him the *V* sign and raged, 'Up yours WANKER!' causing a few looks from a passer-by.

I trudged further on, and for some reason the local library seemed inviting. I gazed at my digital watch; it displayed two-thirty pm on it. I thought to myself seeing that I had got nothing better to do at the present time I might as well pay this establishment a visit. Inside I idled some time away. I now knew that I must find another job or I would become a new statistic to the unemployment figures that week, which I did not find appealing. I looked around in the business section, a book caught my eye, and the title written on it had the words: *How To Set Up Your Own Business With Government Funding*. I know the title sounded distinctly cheesy but I pulled this piece of literature out and flicked through a few pages.

'Mmm well this seems interesting, maybe it will give me some ideas to work with,' I thought out aloud. As I turned around my head still buried in the book, I bumped into a scruffy smelly tramp; he must have been stepping behind me. He dropped the book he held while staring at me with a spaced out expression; the tramp managed to speak a few slurred words.

'You knocked me on purpose.' He then spat on the floor before staring back up at *me*. My nose twitched due to the tramp's offending odour. I told him that I was 'sorry.' His eyes came up right close to mine and he spoke some more threats aggressively:

'Come on son. I'm pissed. I'm psychotic; I'm ready for all challenges. Do you know I have the power to destroy you with remote viewing - *Eh*! what do you think of that?'

'I'm sure you have, now get out of my way, or I will put you down. I'm not in the mood for this today!' A couple of people moved their heads over in our direction with concerned looks. Me and the tramp then started to shove each other, next we positioned ourselves to square up for an inevitable punch up. I angrily proclaimed for this piece of 'smelly humanity' to get out of my way. I threw a punch that luckily for me missed, as it would have been down the police station for assault. Luckily a librarian rushed over anxiously telling us both to cool it. The librarian asked the tramp to come with her calling him by his name.

'William! Stop causing trouble.' She beckoned him to follow her. Reluctantly while cursing and mumbling to himself he agreed.

After regaining my composure I took a step forward but my shoe trod on something, I looked down and noticed the tramp had dropped a book. I picked it up and its title struck an inner question that had not been aroused in a few years. The heading on the book was called: *Breakthrough An Amazing Experiment with Electronics To Contact Voices from the Dead.* 'The dead and electronics,' I thought, 'what on earth can this mean?' I read a few pages, which drew my attention to the various electronic languages used in it. The diagrams seemed very simple for someone with my knowledge to grasp. I decided to add this book to the other one I had chosen and took both of them over to the library receptionist who graciously stamped their return dates on the inside covers.

About four o clock I pulled up in my silver Rover car onto the driveway, I could hear my boxer dog Rex barking as he usually did when he heard my automobile near the house. I got out of the car then locked it while carrying some items. I used my worn front door key to let myself into the house; Rex then appeared at the entrance - jumping up with excitement to greet me.

'*Hiya* boy you alright,' I said while trying not to get covered in lumps of saliva or whatever it was that oozed out of the dog's mouth. I called for 'Anna' my wife to see if she was at home. She'd been in the kitchen stirring a pan of stew. Anna came out to greet me planting a kiss on my cheek, 'Have you had a good day?' she asked. I dreaded having to tell her of my predicament, this showed on my face, which now changed into a sunken expression. Anna seemed surprised by my body language, 'What's wrong?'

I sighed in a dejected manner while telling Anna of the events of the day that had now left me without a job or disposable income for the coming month. 'You are in the company of a new member of the unemployment community; I've been fired from my job Anna,' I said.

She replied stunned. 'What! This is a joke isn't it?'

'I'm afraid not, it's definitely fact.'

Anna seemed infuriated and made it plain by getting worked up and annoyed before raising her voice and yelling at me.

'That's great! Now what are we going to do. We can't live off the money I earn as a damn care assistant...can we. Christ almighty Andrew!'

I told Anna to calm down so we could try and discuss things in more depth without sinking into a slanging match.

Rex ran upstairs due to our raised voices, disturbing Tiger, Anna's cat that always dozed off on the top stair at this time of day. He meowed and ran down the stairs. I nearly tripped over the blasted thing and angrily said: 'You stupid damn thing! GIT!' I then gave it a good kick up its backside. It took its revenge by spraying up the wall - I was fuming to kick it again. Anna 'called' for me, I held my gripe with the cat for another day, and went into the living room with agitation instead. Anna had obviously become stressed out, we argued for a minute or so before I sat down beside her trying to allay her fears.

'I'll find a way of getting out of this mess,' I uttered as I put my arm around her, 'there is always someone who wants their TV and video player repaired. It's the in thing now. Don't worry about it. God knows what has happened to this country. The only reason why the firm wanted me out was because they are relocating to the Far East and the labour over there is sweatshop pay. It is as simple as that. Loyalty counts for nothing these days.' We spoke some more before Anna went back to the kitchen to finish preparing off the dinner. I picked up the television remote control and flicked through a couple of channels. I sat back in the brown leather armchair when the sound of something breaking emanated from the kitchen. I asked Anna what she had broken now, but was greeted with a few 'expletive words.' My temper inside of me seemed determined to *reply* back but I thought I'd better not, I had been through enough arguments for one day, and so I pressed the volume button on the television remote to a higher setting instead.

For some reason 'Channel Eight' was broadcasting one of these discussion programs. The subject was about Spiritualism and various other methods of contacting the deceased. A man in the audience grabbed the microphone from the host and started expressing his opinion forcefully:

'I'm not questioning your ability to contact the dead. I'm analysing the methods you claim to use,' he remarked. The audience was beginning to get rowdy with the prospect of two totally conflicting viewpoints clashing. The man stood up and pointed his finger at one of the guests on this 'TV show', who by the sight of her was a lady medium or psychic, well that's what it said on the caption on the screen. The man continued his remarks.

'I'm talking as president and as a scientist, who has studied the Electronic Voice Phenomena for years.' A few jeers rang out loudly from within the audience. I perked up with great interest. That *book* I got from the library was supposed to be about this subject I thought. The man in the audience still babbled on:

'The work of Konstantin Raudive, documented in his book *Breakthrough*...is scientific proof that there is something that can be achieved through the realms of electronic ingenuity. To contact a realm of a dimension, that is invisible to the human senses, and cannot be explained in radical thought.'

The psychic or medium whose name was Dorothy spoke in disapproval, 'The methods that you are suggesting in using I am not disputing! It is that the dimension you are contacting could be low level. You will get earthbound entities plus other malevolent spirits coming through. Now listen they will, or they can take you over. It has been known.' The audience by now was laughing and mocking the woman's answer, they interrupted her with ferocious insults.

'Mmm,' I thought. 'So this is what they are all getting worked up about. According to these people there could be a way with the use of basic electronic equipment to penetrate into a dimension that is invisible and inaudible. But it seems to be dismissed by some people in the Spiritualist community.' Anna gave a shout for me to 'help her with the meal,' the smell revealed it was a chicken casserole she'd been preparing. I quickly switched on my video recorder letting it record the rest of this television discussion programme. My attention had been intrigued by this subject matter. I would be watching the rest of the potential - and scientific questions it presented with interest later that evening.

At eight o clock that evening Anna left for work, I told her earlier we would discuss more ideas about what I was going to do about a job the next day.

Sitting on the bulky sofa in the lounge I switched on my video player and began watching the rest of the television programme about communication with the dead. The subject seemed to be more advanced and varied, video clips were shown of a George W Meek who claimed he'd built a machine to make a two-way conversation with the dead a realistic possibility. A televised segment of Meek was shown *unveiling* his invention to a packed Washington press conference in April 1982. Apparently a certain William O Neil, an electronic engineer and psychic, had made contact with a 'Dr. Mueller' who'd died back in 1969. I watched with a bit of excitement as the video recording of William O Neil talking with this Electronic Ghost was played. He had built a Spiricom device to achieve this, and a number of electronic diagrams were displayed showing how to make the machine. But unfortunately the press conference descended into a shamble as the reporters began to heckle George W Meek and his engineer O Neil about the whole subject. O Neil sat stony faced as certain journalists asked more awkward questions.

One of them called the whole charade 'a cock and bull pretentious fraud.' At that moment I switched off the television and video and sat in silence for a moment. Clouded by a small doubt at what some members of the press asked George W Meek and William O Neil, I myself genuinely believed that maybe this could be the way to make contact with loved ones who'd passed on using some kind of ingenious electronic device. With controlled experiments, this may give a glimpse of what life the personality of the deceased, in its energized state transforms into. This way of thinking was confirmed by Spiritualist mediums claiming a transformation occurs, after the inevitability of physical clinical death.

Chapter 7

Building The Diode Machine

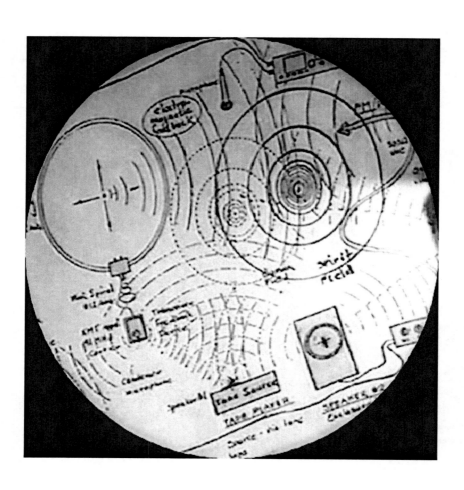

Over the coming weeks I spent a lot of time in my upstairs workshop trying to build a machine that would enable two-way communication with the dead to become possible. I'd obtained many technical diagrams from different books and articles about the 'Electronic Voice Phenomena', plus more complicated literature about this 'Spiricom machine' that George W Meek had been so successful with. Anna not surprisingly was at her wits end due to money problems, and even more annoyed with my obnoxious behaviour, so unfortunately we rowed on many occasions, especially about our dwindling finances, she'd left me twice in the last week alone. But marital problems did not concern me, as finally tonight over much toil and tears I seemed near or enough ready to test my electronic device that I'd constructed. I hoped it would work, and even make me famous or rich.

I slowly looked up from reading the book *Breakthrough*, after studying meticulously the various methods that other people of science used through electronic means to contact the after life.

After a couple of hours I was near enough complete in the assembly of my Diode-receiving device. I soldered two wires to a five-ohms-circuit while placing a two-watt capacitor near the On Off switch. After fiddling about with some wires I was now ready to see if my contraption was going to work. I heaved the large, reddish brown metal encased object upright so it rested towards my view on the reinforced plastic workshop desk. I brushed some coffee stained papers and a bunch of wires onto the floor. I pushed the plug into the wall socket and sat graciously back in my blue leather office chair. I waited a moment then flicked the big yellow switch. Lights on my device flashed erratically, so did the lighting in my workshop. My *eyes* fixated in observation at this Diode device. Between breaths my brain bubbled excitedly, and then in a flurry of electrical power it came on with a burst of loud radio white noise. I clapped my hands in pleasure:

'Well I'll be dammed. The bloody thing actually works!'

I proceeded to connect a big reel-to-reel tape system next to the Diode device, also I attached a large audio wire into the tape recorder from my new machine. I leant over to the wave scope monitor near me and switched it on. The green screen lit up with straight line wave patterns flickering across like a content goldfish on the screen. With all this hand built equipment set up I delved back into the book Breakthrough and at George W Meek's literature about the Spiricom device. I took a deep controlled breath while my mind relayed the many quotations that I'd read.

According to the documentation by Konstantin Raudive in his book Breakthrough, there appears, or so he claims, transmission stations that connect the two worlds with this one. The apparent dimension of the transcendental world of the deceased can be contacted with the proper care.

I would now begin my first experiment into this unknown science. I pressed the large button on the tape recorder and gave out the time and date. The time had approximately 20.24p.m., flashing on my digital watch.

The date was the 26th of February 1985. I 'addressed' the so-called Radio Phoenix station that was supposed to exist dominant like in the world of the unseen. I put on my headphones and held my microphone close to my mouth as I tried for my first contact:

'This is Andrew Stein here calling Radio Phoenix! Can I receive a communication please?'

Nothing happened! So I tried again.

'Stein here calling Phoenix! Can I receive any responses or any communications?'

This session went on for the next forty-five minutes. I kept repeating the same question but got no audible reply. I removed my headphones banging them on my workshop table in frustration. I did not want to believe it, but it seemed I might be becoming cynical to the whole idea of The Electronic Voice Phenomena and that all these precious weeks had been wasted on some stupid practical joke. I stiffened my resolve though, and with the grit of determination pulsating through my veins I realised that I wasn't going to be stopped. Electronic Voice Phenomena was pushing me, controlling me, and forcing me to ignore the *doubts* niggling at me like flies. I wouldn't be stopped from carrying on with this scientific exercise.

I understood that persistence was vital, for before my very eyes I'd watched the video of George W Meek's Spiricom machine actually work like an intelligent robot, and this robot contained the personality from a deceased individual.

'Give up!' I thought. 'Never! Not before trying another relevant avenue of exploration. I must be doing something wrong, this has to be the problem.' My whole mind now seemed captivated and perplexed over this intriguing subject. With renewed energy I paused the tape machine, double-checking to see if it had picked up any voices from the spirit world. Then I checked my Diode device, it made a quiet electrical bleep confirming it still worked.

Thirty minutes had passed when I played the tape back again, but to my dismay I heard absolutely nothing. The recording was blank and had remained in its factory designated silence.

Outside my workshop on the landing my dog Rex got up from his wicker basket situated near the stairs, he scratched to push open my workshop door, obviously I'd disturbed this animal in some way or another. He whimpered then barked as he stepped slowly in. I glanced behind and fumed, 'Flaming hell Rex! What do you want now? For fuck's sake?'

I stood up annoyed at this intrusion, and then shut the workshop door decisively. After sitting back down I decided I would try the experiment one more time.

'If there are no paranormal manifestations this time,' I uttered quietly under my breath, 'Possibly, I will have to confess abject defeat! And if that is the case, I will regard the book "Breakthrough and the science of the Electronic Voice Phenomena and Spiricom a complete fable."' I reset all the equipment and then put my large black headphones on again, squeezing their two synthetic speaker cushions tight against my greasy ears. I began loudly pronouncing my questions again at my Diode machine.

'This is Andrew Stein here calling Radio Phoenix. Please respond?' I shook my head in frustration, 'Come on, damn it work! For God's sake work!' I tried again and demanded in an ever-stronger tone:

'Stein here calling Phoenix! Can I receive some Commu—?' Rex suddenly let out a couple of loud barks - which abruptly interrupted me - he then *stared* around alert.

'Rex,' I said puzzled, 'what's wrong boy?'

To my surprise a strange loud humming noise began to emanate from the Diode machine speakers, and the level indicators began to flicker wildly. I gazed around the room with expectation; the oscilloscope wave machine began to show readings while the numerous needle audio levels on the tape machine went to max. I stood up from my chair pulling my headphones away from my ears with my adrenalin pumping like a steam train. Then a whispering robotic hissing 'voice' began to be heard through the speakers, slowly getting more audible. I struggled to grasp what could be happening. The words spoke phonetically pausing for a moment after each phrase that became audible. Rex cowered to the floor shaking and snarling, his brown hair stood up in a porcupine way, brought about by a fear. I was now certain that something other than my dog must be in the room with me.

The strange voice made the hairs on my neck go static, even though it had not reached its loudest peak yet.

'What's going on?' I whispered. A few tiny orange flashes sparked up from different positions around my electronic equipment, causing a mystical interference to sound out from the tape recorder. A loud knock on the window to the right hand side of me made my senses become rigid. A 'voice' was then heard speaking very clearly:

'I am Natasha. Contact has been established Stein. I am the Mediator!' There seemed a short silence before it continued:

'Turn the voltage selector Andrew? Natasha! Will hold your creative hand!' My precious silver ring on my finger was then gently removed and vanished into thin air by something unseen. I jumped with immense excitement. Next the room started to vibrate a little, so swiftly I put my right hand close to the Diode machine and asked a question:

'Who are you! What are you! A ghost?' My arm started to shake in time to the responding humming sound. Moreover, my expression was one of disbelief and I began to breathe rapidly. Another voice instantly came through, it sounded male or neutral in origin. With slurred tones it announced:

'You have been selected!'

A group of voices whispering and talking in a strange language came louder from my Diode device. I touched it, there next followed a bright flash accompanied by a loud bang that sent my whole body flying backwards bashing into the wall behind me. Rex then growled, and looked at me with nervous *eyes*.

The room was now eerily quiet, except for the sound of the tape machine running. I picked myself up from floor and stood up. I began shaking as I walked cautiously over to my Diode device and tape machine. I checked the tapes to see if anything recorded: it had all recorded perfectly clearly. *I wonder who 'Natasha' is* I thought. I read through some pages of the book *Breakthrough* and other relevant information and could find no connection. I noticed though that Konstantin Raudive had first made contact with someone called 'Spidola', who acted as a mediator on behalf of the transcendental world of the inner dimension, and also the name 'Natasha' was mentioned briefly in his book. 'Was this spirit acting as my own mediator? Which I'd somehow made contact with.' I must have done it I thought. With authority I clenched my fist and shouted:

'YES!'

My excitement coursed through my veins with delight until I was interrupted though by Rex who would not stop jumping up and scratching at my workshop door to get out. I opened the door and Rex run out right down to the bottom of the stairs. I checked the Diode device and other gadgets one last time, then turned all of the equipment off. I stepped out of the workshop room; looking behind me slowly. After that I eyed the walls and the equipment carefully - before switching off the big fluorescent light and firmly shutting the door.

Later that night I lay in bed with Anna beside me in our bedroom. I was tossing and turning but found it quite difficult to sleep. I somehow thankfully managed to lapse back into the world of rest and started to have a weird but strange dream. I found myself staring through my living room window; a dark shadow outline of a female greeted my vision before disappearing. I then could see a dozen or more people scattered about. Because of their recumbent position and lack of movement I realized they were probably 'dead.' They resembled a collection of marble statues in a Greek museum, their faces were grey, the eye sockets empty and dark. Their faces were etched in great sorrow and pain. I passed through the living room window to walk towards and be amongst them. They started to come to life, jostling and pushing me, I barged my way through them and to my surprise they began to melt away like a morning fog. I squinted my eyes and they dematerialized from the scene.

Then suddenly, two familiar people were sitting on two immense red velvet chairs. One of them was my mother, *Cecilia*, who'd passed away three years ago - and for some reason *Stan*, the person who died twenty years earlier. He was sitting beside her. With nervousness I hastened towards them.

'Mother is that you?' I asked trance like. She nodded slowly and turned towards Stan. 'Where have all the statue like bodies gone?' I said.

My mother vanished which immediately left me facing Stan. I asked him the same question again about 'where all the bodies had gone.' He nodded his head and replied, 'They are now all beginning to come into your restful house Andrew.'

I tried to ask another question but I could not speak, a thick blue mist then surrounded me and I could see hands that were yellow and black with decomposition grabbing and scratching me. I saw the figure of Stan laughing, I tried to approach even closer but my lungs were struggling for breath and *I* let out a silent scream. In an instant I found myself back awake in bed but covered in sweat. I sat up for a moment and thought:

'Damn it! Shit! I can't sleep.' I got out of the Queen sized bed quietly; Anna rolled over and groaned as I made my exit to the downstairs. I entered the living room - a stale smell of flowers greeted my nostrils as I switched on the light. I saw the ginger striped Tiger, Anna's cat, lying on the armchair; I stroked him then stared out of the large patio window - similar to the one I'd only just dreamed about. The moonlight night awakened a piece of nostalgia inside of me, while outside in the darkness the wind made the trees rustle as if they were listening to a fateful tune.

'My mother and Stan,' I thought.

'I've had dreams about my mum since her death, but that's the first time I've seen Stan take a part in one in all these years.'

Five minutes went by with myself in reflective mood. I turned away from the window and looked over to my keyboard that stood in the corner near the antique cabinet, a small blue painted china doll given to me by my mother rested with elegance on a glass shelf above it. For some reason I decided that I would perform a song on my musical instrument. Sitting on the piano stool as if I were *Mozart*, I started playing a soothing melody I had written many years ago in my reckless youth. The keyboard I was playing downstairs had now disturbed Anna's sleep. She wondered why on earth her husband took the decision to start making this silhouette of musical notes at this time of night.

Anna got up, putting her oriental patterned satin dressing gown on before leaving the bedroom to find out.

I'd been playing the melody for a few minutes getting myself into full flow when Anna called my 'name.' She was standing by the living room door listening for a minute. I stopped playing and apologized for waking her, Anna smiled and came over towards me, and her big blue eyes reflected the light like two precious crystals. She put her head on my shoulder and kissed me softly on the cheek.

'I've never heard you play that song before. It was really beautiful. Why can't you sleep?' she asked.

'I've been thinking about all the events that have happened over the years Anna,' I replied:

'Merely in the path of reflection do we realize that our life's journey dissolves like dreams we have in our sleep. We dash through our life scratching a living, absorbing the knocks it offers along the way, and we hardly ever pause to ponder the hours. Let alone the days or years, or the people who we leave behind. The many formats that events create have such an impounding effect on our emotions that I wish sometimes I could be removed from the consequences of this merry go round of pain, tears, fear and love.'

'I understand, I've lost my mother and beloved father...plus childhood pets I adored,' said Anna, 'but life moves on its mysterious path and we are dragged along with it. Accepting the fate that deals its *card* to us all. But at least we have each other which is important.'

I held Anna's hand and replied, 'Just as philosophical about life as I am.'

She asked me to come back to bed.

'You go, I will be up in a moment love,' I said. She walked away back to our bedroom. I got up from my keyboard and moved closer to the window one last time. Gazing out in a deep knowledgeable manner my mind deliberated about the experiment I had done earlier and I wondered if I could really be certain that contact may have been made with the spirit world. It triggered a 'question' yearning inside of me; if I could now contact friends and relatives who have died would this bring about a change in my philosophy that dictated my previous actions regarding 'ghosts and religion.' I knew I had to keep trying to gain more information from this Natasha entity or ghost that spoke to me earlier. I had to be precariously discreet, but perseverance might definitely prove me right. I wanted to make sure *I* could achieve a two-way communication with whatever the 'voice' is. Maybe somebody else would come through as well, that would be an added bonus. This electronic science was fascinating and far out - making me wanting to take it much further. I then yawned before retiring back to bed with Anna.

Chapter 8

Strange Occurrences

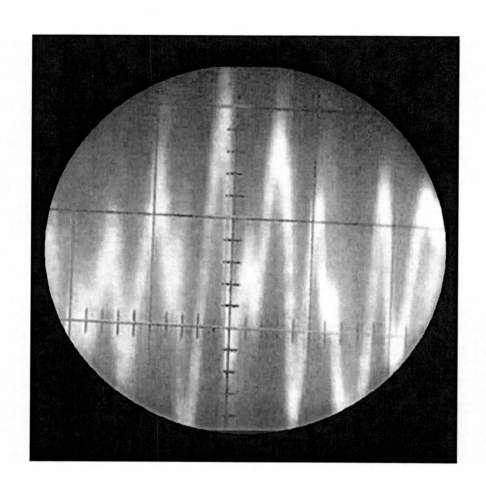

A few more days went by and my conversations with Natasha my 'electronic ghost' wavered between many subjects, they were becoming more defined in their detail. I somehow managed to keep *secret* the worded exchanges this 'entity spoke' away from my wife Anna, until I thought it best to tell her. But other things were now becoming more important. Due to my unemployment and the lack of money coming into the household I knew I had to get a job urgently.

On Thursday in the late morning I talked with Anna about what I planned to do today. We were in the kitchen having a discussion when she gave out a suggestion as she was pulling up the blinds.

'What are you up to today? The bills are piling up and we are falling behind with the mortgage repayments?'

'I will just have a drive around to visit a few people I know. Maybe someone can be of help to me. Hopefully they will be able to throw some work my way,' I said.

'You've been saying them same words for the last seven weeks Andrew,' she retorted. 'I'm fucking sick of this! Come on, why don't you pay Michael a visit.'

I asked her puzzled who Michael happened to be.

'You know, the Michael Pearson guy,' replied Anna with irritation. 'He used to be a work colleague of yours...years ago.'

I perked up.

'Oh yes Mike. I haven't seen him in years. I wonder what he is up to now.'

Anna told me he'd just opened a new 'television and video repair shop' down *Stanley Road* and that she'd noticed the advertisement in last week's local press. She passed the paper to me in a way a teacher would act towards a disruptive pupil, I knew she was losing patience with my arrogance, so I quickly glanced at the address of his shop to avoid a blazing confrontation. I continued reading the local rag for a couple of minutes for extra information on other opportunities. I then assured my wife that I would pay Michael a visit. I kissed Anna on the cheek, rushed into the hallway and grabbed my sheepskin coat and my car keys.

I opened the front door and told Anna that I would see her later on. I was greeted with a few expletive words, 'typical' I thought, so I made my way outside to get into the car parked on the driveway, a safe haven in my opinion away from the wrath of my wife. My mind though still obsessed me; the paranormal recordings that I had been making for the last few nights were virtually implanted in my head like a microchip attached to a computer circuit board, this was the subject I desired to complete. But I needed to concentrate on other pressing matters like a job for instance. I'd got a gut feeling though that today could luckily be very fruitful for my employment prospects.

Later that morning I was driving down *Stanley Road*, when a bastard in a Blue Capri sports car continued crawling up my arse, he'd been doing it for the last couple of miles. The sound of this car's horn really bothered me. The driver of this Blue Capri eventually overtook me as if he was a drunken 'grand prix driver.' I felt a definite road rage, but I was not in the mood for a fucking race with this flashy pillock. I let him go in the end - maybe he would end up killing himself with a bit of luck...I then happened to notice Michael Pearson's sign *written* in large green letters along the front of his electrical shop. I slowed my car down to find somewhere vacant to park nearby. Michael certainly by all accounts had done well for himself by the appearance of his entrepreneur business. I smiled as I was thinking that it would be a 'pleasant surprise' for us to meet again after all these years.

Inside the shop I examined a large 'Stereo Music' unit and a 'Betamax video recorder with a camera.' The prices on them put me off any kind of purchase though. Television devices and other Video equipment littered the display shelves - positioned perfectly to *attract* any unsuspecting customer.

A young spotty faced shop assistant approached me and asked 'if he could be of assistance.' The young person's age I guess must have been about sixteen so I tried acting with some importance to intimidate him.

'Is Mike about? Your boss Mr. Pearson.' The shop assistant stared at me for a few seconds, before telling me he would go and get him.

'Just tell him it's Andrew Stein please,' I said as the youngster made his way into the back of the shop. I could hear some murmuring of voices out the back and I waited with trepidation, abruptly the voices stopped. I then heard someone approaching fast like an over the hill athlete; it was Michael, his mousy coloured hair swept back off his forehead did no favours to his vanity in my judgment, but it was about eighteen years since I'd last set eyes on him. Also the middle ageing process had not seemed kind to him, he stepped towards me and his pasty face lit up with a bemused expression.

'Andrew!' he said as he clasped his hands. 'Andrew Stein! It's great to see you.' He extended his hand and I smiled as we shook warmly.

'All these years,' I said. 'It's good to see you mate. You have certainly done well for yourself, since leaving the electronics company.'

'Too right,' he replied. 'Even though I've struggled immensely, what with the taxes and other annoying red tape. But I think I've made it through the worst period now. I've got this shop up and running and I hope things can only improve. Anyway, how about you and Anna, are you both keeping well?'

I was hesitant with my reply, 'Anna is fine but I'm afraid Michael, I am in a bit of a crisis.'

'What's wrong?' he said.

We were interrupted by the shop door opening and in came an overweight customer who reeked of body odour. Michael 'shouted for Tony,' the name of his young shop assistant to deal with the person. Then Michael invited me to come on through to his office situated at the rear of his shop to recommence our discussion. I did as he asked, following him round the shop counter with enthusiasm and out into the back for a more private meeting.

At my house, Anna continued with the tedious task of having to do the cleaning, Rex our boxer dog was becoming a nuisance constantly getting in the way.

'Out of it please,' she quipped.

She needed to try and feed Tiger her cat with some tinned tuna soon, his favourite delicacy. Anna called his name but there was no sign of the cat. She 'called' again and then entered the living room, looking around all she could see was Rex laying by the dining table.

Anna went upstairs onto the landing still searching but to no avail. My workshop door *drew* her attention though, when she noticed that it seemed to be ajar. This came as a complete surprise to her as the door had always been locked every time I left the house for any length of time. Inside my workshop she could hear strange repetitive sounds coming from within. She gave a curious look, 'Tiger is that you in there?'

Anna treaded cautiously towards the room when suddenly she heard Tiger meowing, fighting, hissing and growling loudly. She ran and pushed open the workshop door to see what could be happening.

The scene that greeted her was shocking. Everything seemed to be happening in a 'slow picture slide motion.' Tiger was fighting with something; it seemed to be another cat but nothing visible greeted Anna's shocked eyes. The Diode machine then came on with the tape recorder, the cat by now seemed devoid of any inhibitions and became more aggressive. Anna put her hand to her lipstick painted mouth. Upset and emotional she yelled:

'Stop it!'

She tried to grab him, but he turned around and scratched her wedding ringed hand deeply, Anna screamed in pain while the cat tore out of the room as quick as a lightening bolt. The Diode machine gave out a kind of robotic sounding laugh, and the brownish red metal box it was encased in made a tapping sound in quick succession, followed by the words:

'You're *next* sweet thing.' The tape recorder then stopped causing the room to have a strange silence.

The workshop began taking a different form, resembling a dark English 14th Century dungeon filled with the sounds of people moaning and crying - this episode began alienating Anna's co-ordination. A small whirlwind blew towards my wife, and then dissipated before everything returned to normal. Anna walked lightheaded closer to the Diode machine, she 'read' the piece of literature lying beside it. The previous evening I'd been engaged in reading a new written article about contacting the dead and the methods of building a Spiricom machine. She glanced confused, and did not understand what this jargon meant, but she'd no time to examine further because downstairs she could hear smashing sounds as Rex and Tiger were fighting each other violently. In a frightened voice she cried, 'What's happening? What's going on, I don't need hassle, I don't need this. Not today!' She ran out of the workshop and tripped over falling to the floor. Getting back up clutching her badly scratched hand Anna ran downstairs.

In the living room there was barking, terrible meowing and hissing sounds coming from within. She could see Tiger scratching and biting Rex. The cat's vicious behaviour resembled that of an extinct sabre tooth tiger. Anna 'screamed' for Tiger to get off the poor dog, panicking she went into the kitchen to fetch a long wooden broom, the sound of precious ornaments smashing were now being caused by the animal's fierce fighting. Anna tried to break up the fight with the large broom which had some success as Rex had now managed to free himself, he bolted out knocking Anna flying - causing her to fall to the ground once again, she lay still for a moment, blood was trickling from her sore scratched hand which dripped slowly onto the blue fur pile carpet.

She looked up. Suddenly to her horror she came face to face with Tiger, *he* hissed and growled as if he was possessed by something, also the animals face seemed to have a blue mist changing its feline features. The 'doorbell rang' but this had no affect on the behaviour of her pet. Tiger's eyes widened, his whole body seemed to expand then his back arched, the cat let out an ear piercing non-human 'evil scream' before sinking its teeth into Anna's make up smudged cheek, she let out a yell in extreme pain as his canines sunk into her delicate skin. The doorbell 'exploded' with a crack as he was prepared to strike out again. Luckily for my wife the phone then rang. This for some obscure reason made the animal start to have a kind of epileptic fit.

At that moment the *picture* of Anna and me taking our wedding vows shattered from on top of the television and fell to the floor.

For some reason Tiger recovered from this fit but something had struck terror into the petrified creature, he jumped over Anna to get to the open living room window. The cat seemed determined to try and make any kind of escape; he desperately climbed up the curtains to find a way out. Anna closed her eyes and touched the bite marks on her face. She then could hear a car outside drowning out the ring sound of the phone. The automobile's wheels were moving with great speed and 80s' rock music blared out from the car's stereo-speakers. Anna was overcome with panic and gasped.

'The road, the car outside, it might run over Tiger.' Anna shot up and rushed to the front door to undo it. At this time Rex slouched upstairs licking his recently war inflicted wounds.

In the approaching car the driver of the Ford Blue Capri called Stuart - who'd smoked cannabis earlier - voiced a few words to his companion.

'I told you Roy. I'll steal extra ganja this evening. Then we will complete the other deal with Cartwright in a few days. This is what life should be about, doing drugs, causing mayhem. Bringing grief to the masses.' He laughed in a wrapped up selfish attitude.

His companion was just about to smoke a joint when he *saw* Tiger sitting directly ahead of the car. 'Stuart! Do that stupid cat! Run it over. I dare you.'

'Alright, lets sandwich it on the road. I'll make it seem more convincing by hitting the brakes. Roadkill! Come on yes! I'm in the mood for this.' Stuart the driver then hit hard on the accelerator.

Anna could see Tiger sitting in the middle of the road. She gazed to the left and witnessed the speeding car. 'Oh my God!' she screamed. 'It's going to hit him.' Anna yelled at the car to 'STOP!' There was then a massive screeching sound of the brakes burning on the wheel cylinders, this caused the tyres to come skidding to a halt. A loud thud that Anna had dreaded to hear entered her jewellery pierced ears, it was too late and she shrieked:

'TIGERRRRRRRR!'

The cat's body lay crushed on the gravel littered road, Anna's beloved pet twitched its front white paw for a second, but it was too late - as the animal had been killed instantly. The car did not stop after its reckless actions and sped off further down the road, the driver Stuart shook his fist in some kind of 'obscene triumph.'

The phone continued to ring within the house, and in a state of shock Anna went inside and into the living room to pick up the receiver. 'Hello,' she murmured. There appeared to be no answer.

'Is that you Andrew?' she asked again trying to hold back her tears. Anna heard a robotic voice address and answer her down the phone.

'Your cat's here with us! Now Anna...you *Cleopatra* hussy.'

Deeply upset and angry she bawled, 'You pathetic sicko. I'm going to report you to the damn police. Fuck you! Do you hear me?' She slammed the phone down hard causing the silver telephone address box resting near the receiver to ping open and empty its pages. Clutching her hand painfully she pulled away the nets and peered through the living room window, outside she saw a couple of neighbours putting Tiger, the now deceased cat, into a black plastic bin liner.

Back at Michael's electrical shop I enjoyed having my cigarette accompanied with a cup of black coffee. Michael and me were in deep conversation catching up on the years and events that happened to both of us. After giving a few choice, or should I say a few 'rude remarks about Mr. Bains,' my old boss at the electronics' factory where I used to work, I explained to Michael that I had to leave or face the sack, the choice to resign, though made with deep regret, seemed right for me in the end.

The caffeine buzz from the coffee I'd drank then made me put a question to Michael to see 'if there were any jobs going in his shop that he could offer me.' Michael made a remark saying 'that his shop was doing quite good business at the present time, and he could use someone with *my* resourceful experience in the TV and video repair field.' My spirits lifted as I would definitely be quite thankful to accept his offer of a job, the money from the work would ease my financial situation and at least it would reassure Anna. Michael and me shook on the *deal* before speaking a few more practical words. I told him that tomorrow he could expect me in to start work.

After I left his shop I decided to go into my local pub for a beer as I had quite a thirst. I'd only been in the pub for a short time when I overheard a couple of people talking about 'a cat' that had been run over earlier down my road, plus an hysterical woman being escorted back into her house. My heart sank.

Oh blast! It can't be Anna's pet they are referring to. Instinctively I left the pub and quickly drove back to my house. When I pulled into the driveway I noticed all the front blue velvet curtains were drawn which seemed strange, so I let myself in the house with the key before I shut the white double glazed door.

'Anna I'm back. Rough and ready. Where are you?' I asked.

'I'm having a bath,' she uttered from upstairs obviously upset.

I walked into the living room and glanced around. I could see some broken ornaments lying on the floor, our wedding photo sat smashed in front of the TV, also a few bloodstains stood out from the carpet's colour scheme.

Anna eventually came downstairs wrapped in a white dressing gown and her eyes were tear-stained, her hand had a bandage wrapped around it and a large plaster was attached to my wife's cheek.

'What an earth has gone on in here,' I exclaimed. 'Looks like a war zone?'

'It's Tiger,' she said mournfully. 'He went completely mad, attacked me and Rex and now he's dead.' I turned to see Rex; he was lying on the floor with a sorrowful face and badly scratched nose.

'Anna, what do you mean, the cat's dead?'

'You heard! He's been run over by a fucking car. He just sat in the middle of the road as if he had a death wish. Tiger somehow escaped through the small window in this room before he ran away as if he was terrified of something. It all started in your workshop.' Anna pulled out a tissue and wiped her eyes. 'I felt weird and confused in there - as If I'd taken drugs. I then chased him into the lounge. He attacked me and bit my cheek. Afterwards he started having a fit or something that I could not explain.'

'Shit! This is all I need,' I said. I undid my shirt collar button and loosened my blue tie - before I examined the broken ornaments and looked at the scattered splintered pieces.

'In respect, any idea on what triggered it?' A look of foreboding crossed my eyes.

'Andrew, when I went upstairs into your workshop I could hear him making a terrible unpleasant racket. He completely went berserk, as if he was fighting with something. But I could see nothing there.' Anna then blew her nose.

My inner voice began raising concerns, causing my perplexed mind to grind over and over in my head.

Now I'd locked the workshop door before I went out that morning. So how did it become unlocked? And how did the cat get in there, I thought. *The experiments that I'd been conducting with the Diode device and the strange paranormal voices that were being captured on the tape were beginning to concern me. Surely there was no connection, it's not that I was using an Ouija board or conducting a séance. The paranormal manifestations were coming from transmission stations from the spirit world, not from inside the house, or were they?* I spoke some words to Anna to try and 'comfort' my wife as best I could.

'Apart from this mess, you will be pleased to know love, that somehow I've managed to secure a job at Michael Pearson's electrical shop.'

'That's something I suppose,' replied Anna in a tension strained voice. Both of us then began cleaning up the mess in the living room as best we could. Afterwards the unpleasant task of having to bury Tiger would be my next chore.

The black sack that he rested in leaned against the back door.

Outside I dug a hole near a fruit tree in our garden and buried him beside it. I put his favourite toy mouse beside him, and gave him a small kiss on the top of *his* head. The rest of him I did not want to see due to the injuries the car had made. It started to rain so I completed my morbid job as quick as I could, I then felt something blow icy air into the arch of my back. I turned around and saw some kind of *large reddish bird* sitting on the fence, a kind of violet glow of light surrounded its body - it 'observed me studiously' for a moment. Next two more strange birds joined it briefly, then they all flew away to a nearby tree. The glow of the moon enlightened the branches to make the tree above me seem alive; I picked up the shovel with a shake in my hands and went back into the house to comfort Anna. She'd been too upset to help me bury her pet.

Anna explained to me that the car, 'a Blue Capri', had driven off when it had run over the cat without any kind of remorse. My conscious enraged with fury, the same car hassled me earlier in the day when I was driving near Michael's shop. I swore if *I* ever found the scumbags they'd be on the receiving end of a right pasting, lets just say it would be their own misfortune if I caught a glimpse of this Blue Capri sports car driving about the town.

Back indoors I thought that we could both do with a drink. I poured myself a large *Napoleon* brandy, while Anna had a double white rum. The drinks were definitely needed after the day's sorrowful events.

Later on in the evening I went up to my workshop without turning the light on, a murky darkness inside greeted my vision, but I could see the oscilloscope was on - and to my surprise I could see the L. E. D. lights flashing on the tape machine. I became puzzled, as I'd turned off all the equipment earlier in the day. I had also locked the door, for some unknown reason though it became unlocked.

I switched on the fluorescent light before moving closer to the devices; I glanced to the floor and could see some of my electronic tools lying scattered about the place, obviously caused by the commotion of when Tiger was fighting in the room. I 'observed the tape machine' and was shocked to find another reel of tape inside of it. It was played half way through with the microphone positioned studio like directly in front of the Diode machine. It seemed like the thing had never moved, despite all the other objects that were on the desk scattered everywhere. I shouted down to Anna to ask her 'if she had touched any of my electronic instruments.' She sternly stated that she most 'certainly did not.' I shut the workshop door and picked a few of my electronic tools off the floor. I decided to play the tape. I put my left hand slowly to my chin, sat down on my black leather chair - before I pressed the large play button. I put my face close up to the tape machine and *watched* intently at the indicators.

Unexpectedly a burst of 'white radio noise' came on very loud. I tried to turn the sound down a bit, but strange noises started to 'scream out' from the tape. It sounded like a feral cat. The sound kept cutting out and flickering back on. I felt an unsettled emotion envelop me; the animal noises on the recording must have been Tiger when he'd been in here. I made some adjustment and could hear Anna's voice shouting on the tape, but it sounded faint due to electronic interference obscuring its tone. My right hand moved to switch the tape machine off, as I did not feel in the mood to listen anymore. I then resonantly heard a 'whispering voice' come through, its sequence of words became more pronounced and it spoke at a quite high audible level. I had no need for my headphones as the sound was coming from the speakers in front of my Diode machine, something that never happened before. I listened carefully as it reached its loudest pitch. I then asked a direct question.

'Can someone talk to me directly, and in a perfect way of acknowledgement to my questions?'

Natasha the electronic ghost came through with her distinct hissing robotic voice. 'Hello Andrew. I'm in the room...I stand in the *Zimmer*!'

I had an uneasy expression, for the first time it seemed possible that I could conduct a two-way conversation with this ghost using only the Diode machine, my heart skipped a beat. I asked a few more questions and Natasha came back with answers.

'Who are you?' I asked. 'What are you? You have told me during our earlier experiments that your voice was coming from a transmission station in the spirit world, and that you were not in my house. Why has this changed? How are you now able to give direct answers - and ask me questions when I speak to you?'

'The link is now strong enough for me to enter your earthbound plane,' Natasha commented in its strange voice. It then continued. 'You have opened an astral-doorway which has allowed me to be in your room.'

My whole being seemed overcome with tremendous excitement, the feeling felt tarnished though with a slight niggling *doubt* troubling me. Abruptly, a male voice interjected with slow pronounced words. 'I fight with cat. He do not like!'

Natasha then came back in with a slow rhythmic question.

'There is someone here who wishes to talk to you... Stein?'

I felt nervous before I acknowledged a reply. 'Who is it?'

There came a brief silence before my query was answered.

'Andy boy, it is me. Stan!'

I shook my head while giving a *serious* look. 'Stan is that really you. Do you really survive death?'

A creepy long pause greeted me before Stan pronounced some extra words. 'I smoke my pipe. I need tobacco, I can have anything I like, I can see you Andrew. I am in the room with you.'

'You are in the room with me Stan, how can that be? Are you not speaking from a spirit transmission station?'

His tone and attitude then 'entirely changed' and he talked completely out of character with the *Stan* I had once known.

'Can't I even get through. You flaming bastard, you skunk!'

'Repeat that again. I don't understand your meaning,' I said disturbed.

'I hated... Glad!'

It paused, then he, or whatever it was spoke something else regarding his appearance while he'd been alive on earth. His description he gave was completely untrue. He described himself as being tall and well built, in his 40s with thick brown hair and had died in a traffic accident. This again was wrong as the Stan I knew died from old age and complications from a fall while being attacked. Also his 'comments about Glad' his sister did not make rational sense, as Stan loved his sister, mind you they did have barmy discussions and rows when I lived with them.

Another male voice with an unpleasant threatening tone addressed me. 'We are *all* in your house Stein. We see you!' I ignored this different male voice and I put another question to this

Stan personality, the answer back again did not add up. These questions seemed to be annoying him and it spoke to me again.

'Andrew you're stupid. I speak, you can't hear me diabolical fool!'

I gave a loud rebuff reply back to it. 'You are not Stan, only someone who is impersonating him.'

The Stan voice then cut out and the Natasha personality, or whatever else it might have been reacted back in hatred.

'I am the *Devil!* Here we love not a soul. I pick fight. I come to house, I will possesses you.' It screamed these sentences in a way a lunatic might babble if trapped in a mental asylum. A hissing laugh followed up, coming from my other would be antagonist Stan. I now really wanted to end this experiment, as I felt mentally drained.

'I have no interest in your kind anymore,' I protested.

Natasha came back with an angered voice. 'Do not turn the Diode machine apparatus off or it will cut off our conversations, they will come to an end. Do you understand me Andrew? Do you understand me? There is no such thing as *time* over here. I can see your future Andrew - do not display your naivety.'

I decided 'enough is enough' with the experiment and switched the machine off. There followed a faint robotic sounding scream accompanied with a laugh before everything became silent. I shivered as if someone had stepped over my grave; the thoughts occurred to me about what the 'hell I'd got myself into.' I touched the Diode machine again and my hand shuddered, as it felt ice cold. The feeling was a similar sensation I'd experienced earlier in the garden. I took a pen and wrote down on my notepad what I'd just been through. I thought about the sphere or place where the voices speaking to me might be coming from, now having fuelled my adventurous nature further.

The two-way conversation had now been achieved just as George W Meek and William O Neil's Spiricom device claimed to have done. But the queries I asked Stan confused me further. I graciously asked him relevant questions to begin with, but his comments back, were totally out of character and incorrect, though they did justify that I might be talking to someone else in a discarnate unseen world. The Natasha character also preyed on my mind, as it seemed to be building a unique hostile approach to me, especially when I dismissed the character impersonating the Stan I used to know twenty years ago. Feeling a tad uneasy I switched off all of the equipment, and made sure I locked my workshop door before I exited.

A couple of nights later Anna and me were sitting up in bed with the portable television on. 'Séance In An Old Rag and Bone Yard' from 'Steptoe and Son' was being shown: a BBC comedy show from the 1960s - ironically it had been Stan's favourite. A very strong wind blowing outside made the bedroom windows rattle like skittles and the trees outside swayed about as if deathly phantoms were travelling amongst them.

My eyes were reading a couple of books about the 'Spiricom device' and 'Trance Mediums'. I'd not been in my workshop for two days as I was too scared to enter. The feeling of doubts and my pensive imagination insisted on spinning around in my brain - creating all kinds of strange weird sounds and morbid images.

Anna's usual bottle of Bacardi and the phone rested on a small table by the side of the bed, and she took to drinking another glass of the stuff; irritated by my reading and drunk and erratic she badgered me. 'You haven't said much tonight, what is the matter with you?'

I ignored her, for my mind was deeply engrossed in my books. Anna became restless with me - making it forcefully known. At that moment the bedside lamp flashed on then off. I put my book down and answered her. 'Come on Anna, problems! I'm trying to concentrate.' Laughter from the television show peaked in the background and Anna became more worked up. She began telling me not to be anarchic with *her* - the alcohol seemed to be having a negative affect as well. 'What is that book you are reading?' she said. Instantly she grabbed it from my hands. I asked her to 'give it back' but she ignored me, she flicked through a few pages causing her face to become disturbed.

'What's this bullshit you are reading? Electronic communication with the dead! Mediums! Life after death, I don't believe this. Have you gone completely mad! I also saw pages about this in your workshop the other day? Well. Give me an answer!'

'Anna you have not got a clue about the subject, don't query my motives, I'm just interested in these unexplained sciences,' I replied. The cream coloured phone began to ring interrupting our altercation, Anna picked up the receiver:

'Hello,' she said. Silence greeted her from the phone. 'Hello who is this?' Still silence. A burst of static electricity then entered into Anna's hand from the phone causing it to drop from within her grasp. 'Frickin' hell! Andrew, there's something wrong with the phones, I've just felt an electric shock.' Anna rubbed her hand against the golden duvet to ease the discomfort. 'This is the second time - some unknown prankster has phoned us. I'm getting sick of this.' She then had a 'thought' come back to disturb her. At the moment before Tiger got run over by the Blue Capri car, the phone rang. When she answered it after witnessing the horrible event, a strange neutral robotic sounding voice 'addressed her' in a menacing way with the words:

Your cat is here with us now, plus an insulting term to accompany it. She'd just been about to say something about this to me when the sound of Rex barking distracted her.

'Great,' I said. 'Now the dog has started, I will have deal with him.' I upped from the bed and walked out of the bedroom.

As I stepped onto the stairs landing the light dimmed before cutting out. I tried the switch but nothing happened, I moved on further when all of a sudden Rex's barking stopped. Then a 'massive bang' sound caused the house to shudder. The portable television in our bedroom fell off the table by its own accord. Anna got out of bed and started angrily shouting at me about what the 'hell was happening.' I became suspicious about the whole events that were unfolding.

I could hear the barking again but it seemed to be coming from the inside of my workshop. Anna stood by the bedroom door opening; I put my arm behind me in a gesture telling her to stay behind me and not to shift. I could then *see* a faint blue mist coming from my workshop door, this was followed by the sound of a click, and it had been unlocked. The barking sound then intensified from the workshop's interior. I could not believe my eyes or ears about what could be happening. I thought this drama must be all nonsense. I felt an impulse *push* me - and I rushed to the door to open it. Staring hard into the darkness I could see nothing.

I called out: 'Rex is that you in here?'

Complete silence occurred when I announced my dog's name. The tape recorder came on for some reason and to my great fear, the Diode machine also powered up to function. Now I concluded that it might be best to make an escape, as I had no idea about what I might be dealing with. For some reason I shivered and froze, a massive flash and lots of static electricity surrounded my head, I put my hand over my ears but I stumbled - falling with dread into my workshop. Anna 'shouted my name,' but before I could respond, the workshop door slammed shut with amazing force. Anna ran to the door trying to open it.

Lying on the floor wearing a blue dressing gown I felt disorientated. In my workshop darkness surrounded me, except for the numerous L.E.D. lights flashing on the tape machine and the Diode device, these being the only source of light. A strange electrical charge punctured the room with an overwhelming odour. I could hear Anna outside calling my name while banging on the door. I moved my head slightly and in a frightened tone I asked:

'Show yourself! Who is there?'

Natasha, in her ghostly whispering robotic *voice* replied back to me from about half a metre away from my unkempt face.

'I do a good impression of your dog, don't I Andrew! How do you like being in the dark with *us?*' Her word's had menace, and were followed by a number of blue flashes. I struggled to get up, a dark shadow flashed past me making all of my hair on the back of my neck stand on end. Next I could feel a cold sensation *touch* the right hand side of my face. Anna was frantically twisting and turning the workshop door handle, panicking she called out my name:

'Andrew!'

Anna then tried banging the door with her hands in intense desperation. This caused her injured hand scratched by the now dead Tiger to start to bleed again.

Back within my workshop I could hear a 'ghostly voice' speak right into my *ear.*

'Stein it's me, Stan, I'm in the room. I don't need your damn machine to make contact with you anymore.'

I screamed around for the Stan personality to 'get out!' One thing now terrified my senses. The conversations I had with these spirits or electronic ghosts only came from the Diode device and tape machine, now this thing or entity was actually speaking without the aid of any electrical equipment. This was never achieved in the so-called books about electronic methods to contact the dead. I shouted once more at the thing to 'leave' and at that moment Anna finally managed to get the workshop door open. I made my dash for the exit with a few sparks following me as I made my way out of this bewildering room. Anna's emotions were distressed and I must admit I was badly dazed by the experience I'd just been put through. Anna asked if I felt okay, and then spoke further anguished words to me. 'Something is going on in there Andrew. Tiger knew it, and now it has happened to you.'

I did not dare tell Anna about what I had just experienced in the workshop, the shock could have affected her nerves that were already unstable due to the cat dying and the large amounts of alcohol she'd been consuming in binge fashion. I composed myself as best I could and I told Anna that 'no one' must go in there until I could find out what the hell was going on.

Without warning Rex came running upstairs and began barking at the workshop entrance furiously. A scratching noise coming from the floor in front of my wife and me could be heard quite emphatically. This seemed to be the trigger to cause Anna to shake with fear. The events, the drink, and the lack of sleep finally overwhelmed her and she started to lose *control*. Rex continued barking feverishly. I grabbed Anna and told her to 'calm down!' But she began to cry and started hitting me with her bloodstained hand. I shook her firmly and told her to get a grip.

'Stop it! Anna now. STOP ITTTTTTTT!' She then began weeping. I placed her head on my shoulder and wrapped my arms around her, holding her close. I glanced up towards the workshop and its closed door - feeling propelled with anger and distrust. I rested my head against the distressed and shaking Anna and took a deep breath.

An hour later the 'Blue Capri' sports car, the contributor to Anna's beloved cat's demise - drew to a stop down the bumpy deserted *Shackleton Road*, eighteen miles from the nearest town. Its headlights remained on ready to be recognized.

'Just park here Stuart, nothing fancy. Cartwright is supposed to meet us in ten minutes.'

'I still don't like this idea of yours though,' said Roy with anxiety.

'Be calm mate, everything is arranged for the deal to take place shortly.' Stuart's sentence had a zealous undertone.

Gradually, two bright lights like a Good's Truck headlamps approached the back of the 'Blue Capri' rear window.

'That should be him, leave it to me,' said Stuart. At that moment, the bright lights vanished and the headlamps of the 'Capri car' blew up causing the two partners in crime to quake in fear. A mundane claustrophobic darkness then encased around the windscreen and passenger windows causing a sensation of intolerable isolation.

'What the fuck is going on?' screamed Roy. 'I wanna leave now! Cartwright's double-crossed us, can't you see. We've been set up all along. Move It!'

Stuart thumped the dashboard in response and tried turning the ignition key, but it became red-hot - searing into the flesh of his hand.

'Argggghhh,' he yelled.

Roy tried the passenger door and an enormous electrical shock went into his muscle causing the arm to snap in two with a sickening break of the forearm bones. The pain he experienced caused him to let out a desperate 'cry of mercy.' Then the car started to shake with forceful pressure, moving from side to side. Stuart felt scratch marks tear into his body causing his designer green 1985 sweatshirt to shred. Blood poured out of the wounds being inflicted. He struggled to fend off this unexplained invisible violent attack. An orange mist accompanied with an electrical humming noise then materialized into the back seat of the car, its character resembled that of an old man. Roy turned his head behind him and then felt a slicing pressure around his neck.

'My throat. Don't kill me!' he pleaded.

A yellowish ghostly leather hand panned along with deliberate movements, creating a momentary paralysis, then the neck snapped, causing Roy's immediate death. His partner, Stuart, continued to have his body scratched violently, accompanied with two strange *occult symbols* being burnt onto his wound inflicted chest. He put his hand onto the condensation filled windscreen and tried writing the words *"Save us"* with his bloodstained finger. Stuart let out one more 'scream' before passing out, eventually to die due to the ferocity of the attack. The orange unearthly mist then fully formed on the back seat of the car, the old man became a solid object. It smiled with disturbing indifference after completing its macabre task. The ghostly entity figure was an imitation of Stan. *It* remained still for a moment then vanished, ready for its next course of action.

Chapter 9

Strange Forces

After the events that had happened in the workshop and the death of Tiger I sent Anna away to her sisters for a week to get some kind of rest for her mental state. During her period of absence - dealings in the house seemed normal, no more strange voices or noises were heard. Mind you, I did always have a fear in the house during the dead of night of being alone, and made sure Rex slept on the end of my bed.

Anna returned back home after being away at her sisters and seemed more calm and relaxed. I said goodbye to her before I left for work at Michael's that Tuesday morning. I'd fixed another strong lock on my workshop door, also I tried my best to make sure all the equipment stayed off, especially the Diode machine. A main trip-switch that supplied all the power for the workshop was re-routed into a small fuse box under the stairs.

Later in the morning at Michael's electrical shop I'd just finished doing a repair job on a television. I put down my screwdriver then read the time on my watch. Michael who was working on a video recorder suggested that a 'tea break' seemed due.

'Mike,' I asked in a broad fashion. 'I've got to talk to you about something.'

'Sure friend,' he replied. 'Lets just settle down properly on this bloody rickety stool. Right I'm all ears.'

'This might sound a bit weird coming from me, but I want you to try and be objective.'

'I doubt that, but go on,' said Michael as he took a sip from his coffee, a curious expression etched on his face.

I lit a cigarette then took a deep puff. 'Did you ever hear of the scientists *Konstantin Raudive, George W Meek* or *William O Neil* - or ever read any of their books?' I asked.

'Yes I remember that William O Neil. He built a machine to help him talk to a cranky ghost on the other side. I've always been fascinated on how he ever achieved this.'

'Well you may not believe what I am about to say, but I have achieved the same results by building my own Diode machine.' My tone of voice struggled to dampen my boasting ego.

'Wow! Wow! Wow! Andrew. You're going right off the deep end. No one, I mean no one was ever able to achieve the same results "William O Neil got."' Michael considered for a moment and then continued. 'I recognize something though, about the subject you are going on about. I recall at various stage in the seventies "Konstantin Raudive" pioneered work using tape machines, radios, a Diode machine, and a Psycho-phone to contact the dead. But I never knew what the hell a Psycho-phone could have been. I suppose it's just one of the many electronic devices he used in his research.'

'Say Mike,' I remarked. 'I've been trying out my own EVP experiments using the method's written in different books. Do you wanna bear witness.' I then pulled out with delicacy a couple of cassette tapes and asked Michael to play them. Michael with a negative attitude restraining him hesitated, but eventually he did what 'I asked' and he began to listen intently. The tape started to slow down and speed up a little, and a strange humming noise slowly filtered out from the speakers. The ghostly robotic voice of Natasha talked and also the voice of the ghost pretending to be

Stan. Michael's face squinted slightly as he tried to make sense of the ghostly voices. I was about to speak but Michael asked me not to interrupt. The tape continued for a minute longer then stopped with a pop. Michael sat in stony silence for a while trying to make some kind of rational sense of the voices he'd just heard.

'What do you reckon then?' I commented with pride.

Michael pondered for a moment in thought. 'I don't know Andrew. There is definitely something there. But I'm baffled about the content.'

'You see, I told you ghostly voices are on there.'

'There is,' noted Michael. 'But what do you mean it could have been ghostly messages? It might have been something as irrelevant as a C.B. radio, or Walkie-Talkie - or another kind of radio frequency transmission.' Michael's brow furrowed for a moment. 'Nevertheless if you want to take my qualified advice. If you are getting signals from wherever these voices claim to come from, you are better off stopping it. At once!'

I gripped Michael's blue work overall and exclaimed: 'I'm too involved with it now. It's like a drug. Anyone with an ounce of desire and armed with this equipment can contact a dimension from which discarnate spirits can actually speak. We can communicate with people from the other-side. Electronically!'

'Look Andrew!' reiterated Michael. 'Leave this shit alone! I had a mate who dabbled with a Ouija board once - and he ended up being sectioned to a psychiatric institution, his mental health in ruins.'

'Don't dare make comparisons with this science and the same old crap about ghosts and poltergeists. Nothing can harm me,' I snapped. Then abruptly I stuttered to a halt. The 'Nothing can harm me quote' I'd said rested uneasily on my mind. For the first time in my life I believed in ghosts and was beginning to wonder about my own sanity in getting involved with this subject, especially after the events that had happened while I conducted sessions in the workshop. I knew I could not 'dismiss Michael's poignant question.' I took another drag on my cigarette and Michael asked me if everything was all right at home with Anna and me.

Doubtfully I said, 'Yes.'

'Come on,' shot Michael, 'out with it! Is it anything to do with this crap you are playing about with?'

I let out a heavy sigh before deciding to tell him the full extent of the events that had happened in the workshop over the last few days. 'Look mate, ever since I conducted these experiments there has been a couple of incidents that I can't explain. You know our cat Tiger has died.' Grief briefly touched my voice.

Michael acknowledged in sympathy.

'Well Rex, my dog, has acted strangely and the other night I felt as if there could be something *in* the workshop with me. My gut reaction told me it must be something sinister. It talked right into my ear. Now what with this and the stress it has put on Anna and our relationship I wish I could just turn the whole darned thing off. Oh this is silly Michael.' I finished the rest of my cigarette before concurring further about the contacts I'd experienced with Stan and Natasha – all talking through this Diode machine I'd built.

Michael tried to bolster me and asked me to leave the tapes with the ghostly voices on it with him. He told me he would check up on various textbooks that fortunately were in his possession on this paranormal subject. He'd also, with more time at hand, try and run a number of advanced tests on the tapes. 'Don't worry Andrew,' hinted Michael. 'I will speak to someone I know who'll have informed knowledge and a greater *expertise* than me on this whole subject matter.' He slapped me on the shoulder like a best mate. Next we heard a few 'shouts' coming from the shop and Tony the shop assistant came in telling us that a 'Mr. Rodgers' had brought his television back again with a complaint about the shoddy work done on it.

'Shoddy! Bloody cheek!' groaned Michael. 'Now I've got to go and deal with this same burke again. I told the moron not to touch the vertical hold switch. He's probably fused the tube!'

I chuckled as my annoyed friend went out to confront this irate customer.

Back at my house later on, Anna was listening to classical music playing on the Hi Fi. She'd sat down relaxing on the sofa as the early afternoon passed by. The doorbell sounded and Anna went to the front door to open it. Carol the next-door neighbour's wife stood there - and she held a few music records in her arms.

'How are you, Anna,' she said. 'You doing okay? I've brought a few of my L Ps I own. I thought you might like to borrow them. They're my favourites.' Carol gave Anna the records and then relayed important news told to her by a friend with a direct source to the Police. 'By the way, I've got information that could be of interest.'

'What news do you have?' asked Anna.

'Well you know that *car* that killed Tiger.'

'Yes the Blue Capri.'

'Well for reasons that are unbeknown to me, a Blue Capri was found down a dirt track off *Shackleton Road* with the driver and his companion...Dead as doornails. Both trapped inside. There is a sting in the tail to this strange crime though. I've been informed by the police, that they suspect both were killed by some kind of perverse maniac, due to the horrific scratch marks found on one of the bodies, and the broken neck injury on the other one. Also, bloodstained lettering written on the windscreen formed the words *SAVE US*.'

'You mean they were...murdered!' said Anna with torrid unease.

'That's correct,' responded Carol. 'But the puzzling thing bothering the Police investigation is that all the car windows and doors were locked from the inside, with no sign of any ignition keys. The scene of the crime at this moment is still crawling with CID detectives. This is what I heard on good authority from one of my friends who works at the local Police station's admin department.'

Anna felt disturbed by the events Carol had explained to her, however, she did not show these emotions. For company, Anna invited Carol into the house and they shared a cup of coffee. They watched the local TV news broadcast. The announcer, without much detailed information confirmed the 'murders' briefly. Both women talked some more about this subject and other gossip making its rounds from the local town.

After an hour or so, Carol explained to Anna that 'if she didn't want to be alone, all she had to do was contact her and her husband John next door.' Anna was grateful for this and when they'd finished chattering a few minutes more - Carol left the house.

In a secret conversation earlier, *I'd* asked John and Carol to keep an eye on Anna while I was away at work. Although Carol had not helped the situation by blurting out the reports of what happened to the driver and his companion of the Blue Capri. *I'd* already known about these bastards' demise - and felt quite happy in a way to see a couple of scumbags get their just deserts, although due to misconstrued third-party information, the manner of their violent deaths had not been relayed accurately to me.

Anna went into the kitchen for a glass of water then headed back into the living room. She read through the titles of Carol's records and decided to put a soothing classical disc on the Hi Fi. She took a deep breath before sitting down on one of the luxury armchairs. Anna smiled and listened to the music's dulcet tones fill the room. She closed her eyelids and drifted off to sleep.

A couple of hours later and darkness swept away the afternoon's sun. Anna's eyes blinked open and she woke up feeling relaxed. Rex sat on the leather couch and she thought it best to let him out into the garden. As she got up the 'phone rang.' Anna pressed the light button before going over to pick up the phone. Suddenly the room seemed to have a growing tension in it - maybe the reason for this was due to the sound of the phone ringing - or maybe it was something to do with the record player's turntable. The Hi Fi had not stopped for some reason and continued playing the disc: the stylus kept repeating back on the empty end groove of the record.

Anna slowly yawned, flicked her hair back and put the phone close to her ear. 'Hello,' she murmured, silence greeted her. Her lips dried. She then spoke again. 'Hello is anyone there?' Anna could hear a ghostly singing voice speaking her 'name.' It became more audible and repeated her name like an echo.

'Anna! *Anna. Anna. Anna!*'

'Who is this?' she asked.

Anna felt a static click brush against her plaster patched cheek, then the line went dead. Anna gazed at the handset examining *it* briefly. She stared around the room curiously then like a shock the Hi Fi record started playing music followed by a few green sparks coming from the stylus' arm. Unexpectedly, and to her surprise, the Hi Fi power ceased causing the room to be devoid of any sounds. Before Anna could react to this she heard a 'voice' coming from upstairs in a loud and distinct ghostly tone.

'Anna! Come play with us!'

Rex became alert and barked, his short brown hair on his back stood on end. Anna could still hear this strange voice and stepped slowly out of the living room and stood by the bottom of the stairs. She peered up into the oppressing darkness and turned the landing light on. Walking slowly upstairs to where the sound of this voice might be coming from, she glanced briefly at the photographic pictures hanging on the wall; they seemed to impact conflicting memories of times gone by.

Anna reached the top of the landing situated near the white painted staircase and nervously stepped to my workshop door, putting her sensitive ear up against it. She could hear nothing. Anna tried the door handle but the door was firmly locked by myself.

Anna moved slowly along the landing to the large square window - an old man, his body lit up by the large 1950s' streetlamp on the road graced past the house catching her eyes and attention. Anna stared *intently* at him, the old man stopped, turned and his eyes connected with Anna's. The man was wearing a black uniform, similar to that of a 'German Nazi SS officer' would have been dressed in if the time period had been World War II. Three other people ran quickly past and the old man vanished when these people moved through him. Anna's feelings were compounded with nervous perceptions. Then my keyboard began playing downstairs, the notes it performed were moulded into the style of a 'perverse weird orchestral opera.' She looked over her shoulder in a slow uneasy fashion. The old man who'd been out on the road then reappeared, the bottom half of his legs below the knee faded away enabling him to glide to the front of the house. Anna could hear a ghostly hissing voice speak. It announced:

'WE ARE IN YOUR HOUSE!'

Frightened and disorientated Anna's whole senses then became rigid. The old man whose appearance was cleverly disguised by the ghost-entity imitating Stan instantly levitated up the front of the house and his ghostly face closed right up against the upstairs landing window. Then there was a loud bang, this was the signal for the living room door to slam shut trapping Rex in there. Anna jumped clockwise around in a hypnotic state towards the landing window, to her horror she came eyeball to eyeball with this ghost entity. The entity's face with its malformed features pressed up hard against the window. Anna's vision met the ghost's and her *eyes* began to widen and enlarge with terror. The ghost's face morphed into a chalky white colour and its mouth opened to reveal its contents.

It was slimy black in colour and the word 'Stan' resonated out of it. Anna tried moving but she was paralysed with fear, she vainly wanted to 'scream' but her voice would not respond. The face and expression of the ghost turned to one of evil hate etched on to it.

Rapidly a dark hooded figure appeared behind Anna and began to get closer before vanishing. She felt an icy breeze blow through her long brown hair and an air of paranoid unreality engulfed her. Then the hands of the ghost outside the house reached through the glass and grasped Anna around her head; they were yellow, grey and clammy in colour - and were covered in an orange covered fluid. Anna managed to shake her head free and finally let forth a scream in terror.

'NO! HELP MEEEEEEEEEEEE!'

Driving in my car approaching the house I noticed with my headlamps on Anna standing extremely close to the upstairs landing window. She was bashing her hands up against it. I pressed hard on the car brakes causing it to skid and screech to a halt. Unknowing of the events taking place I tried opening my car door in the usual casual fashion when the central locking device activated and I became locked in. *I* now knew something must be seriously wrong.

As a despairing witness my eyes could see Anna in her distress and I began to panic. I noticed an orange shaft of light hovering near the window where my wife was. I tried to wind down my window but it would not budge, I banged my fist on the steering wheel with anger. I had got to do something, so I took hold of the steering lock and smashed one of the car's windows with it. At that moment the interior car light brightened up before exploding like a dazzling firework. I somehow managed to struggle out of the window opening to get out. Extremely shaken I hit the ground causing a graze to my elbow. John my neighbour dressed in pyjamas came from inside his house due to all the commotion. As I struggled up I screamed:

'Anna! Anna! What's happening? WHAT IS HAPPENING!!!'

Anna seemed hysterical, flailing her arms about in acute distress.

'Andrew! Help. Me!' she cried.

I ran over to the front door and in panic tried to get my keys out of my pocket. Anna continued 'screaming' and banging on the window. I put my key into the front lock but to my horror the door was locked from the inside. My cut hands covered up to my face briefly before I screamed:

'No! What the fuck is going on!' Filled with fear and rage I began to violently smash the door with my shoulder.

John my neighbour sprinted over to me extremely agitated. 'What's this commotion about,' he said with nervous breaths. 'Sounds like someone is being killed?'

I turned to John in a state of panic. 'I think someone, an intruder is in the house. We have got to get this door open.'

'Jesus Christ!' John then helped me with getting the locked door knocked down. Rex was barking furiously inside the lounge and knocked a couple of chairs over, he also, due to fright, chewed in a wolf like manner into the carpet - causing small ripped holes to accumulate.

Carol, John's wife stared out of her dimly lit bedroom window in an anxious disposition. I noticed Carol, and shook my head. Then my temper flipped due to the locked door. 'Come on! Come on!' I yelled. The door, which John and I were forcing, seemed to take an eternity before it finally opened due to the strength of the both of us. Immediately I tore into the house, running upstairs and shouting angrily.

'Get away from her! You Bastard. Stay away from my wife!' Upstairs I rushed to Anna, pulling her away from the window, she was shaking and in shock. I hugged her tightly against me but Anna told me not to 'touch her.' I shouted downstairs to John to check the rest of the house and make sure everything was secure. Anna's eyes were still *transfixed* on the window, but the ghostly intimidating figure of Stan had disappeared, it had melted away like a *Victorian London* night mist. Anna then began sobbing.

'It was going to get me. It was going to kill me if it got into the house.'

I tried to calm her down as best I could. 'What was going to get you?'

She backed away from me with her eyes dazed and distant, she kept muttering the same words. 'The ghost tried to attack me. It was horrible and it had a name.'

'Anna what is its name?' I asked. 'You must tell me. It is most important.'

John my neighbour shouted up to me to say the house was now made 'secure.' He'd put our dog Rex into the garden to stop any more damage being done to the living room. John also stated he could find no evidence of an intruder. I thanked him and told him he could go back home. I turned back to Anna and repeated my question about the name. Stuttering and still in distress she uttered the answer:

'S…St…Stan.' Then screaming with tears running down her face she declared: 'There is something in this houseeeeeeeee!' She buried her head on my shoulder for some kind of comfort and this seemed to ease the disturbed emotions eating away at her. I closed my eyes and knew that the experiments I'd been conducting with my Diode machine to contact the dead, had undoubtedly set free an electronic paranormal phenomenon, thus gaining a momentum of its own nature which I could no longer control. With hindsight there was no doubt that I'd unleashed some kind of force.

Could I give a rational explanation on how this manifestation of Stan, who had died years ago, had been able to appear in full view of my wife? I'm afraid I could not! It was so perplexing for my battered intellect to grasp.

After a kiss and a hug, my wife and me went slowly downstairs into the kitchen. I telephoned the doctor asking him to 'come to the house' to check out Anna. After a forceful altercation he finally agreed to my wishes. Still deeply worried about my wife, the doctor finally arrived an hour later. He attended to her and carried out a short examination to see if Anna was going to need a stay in Hospital. I deeply feared that I could send my wife 'nuts' with the events happening due to these paranormal experiments *I'd* done. The presence of misfortune seemed to hasten towards me at this point of time.

I repaired the front door while the doctor spoke some medical terms to Anna. About twenty minutes later I waited for him to come into the hallway.

'Mr. Stein,' he said. 'I have given your wife thirty milligrams of diazepam. And in addition, ten milligrams of Stelazine, it's an anti-psychotic drug with sedative tendencies. She is on the sofa resting. She should be calm for the time being and may sleep deeply through the rest of this night.'

'Is she going to recover doctor?' I asked. 'Because you mentioning anti-psychotics gets me worried.'

'Mr. Stein,' said the doctor. 'In my opinion your wife might be suffering from severe stress. Let me try and get to the point quickly. Can you take my deliberation, for what it is worth? It's about substances. Now is she, or are you taking any kind of street drugs?'

'What's that supposed to mean? Of course we don't!' I shot back furiously. 'What do you take us for! A couple of idiots! And why did you want to know if I do drugs?'

'Calm down Mr. Stein, I didn't mean to imply anything awkward. I just wanted to know - for my own curiosity. That's all.' The doctor then gave some stern advice. 'I think it's best that your wife comes into my surgery in the near future. I may have to refer your wife to a local psychiatrist for assessment...Now forgive me for asking one last question - as your wife wouldn't tell me accurately. But what made Mrs. Stein become hysterical?'

I thought it best not to tell him the complete truth and just explained that a 'car had killed our cat' and this affected her quite badly. The doctor closed his bag and bid me goodnight as he stepped out the front entrance towards his light blue Mazda car. I shut our damaged front door and rested my head in relief against the large wooden board nailed to it. I hoped Anna did not relay to the doctor the things she witnessed that evening, he might have been tempted to put her away in a mental institution. Also why he brought up the subject of drugs unsettled me. For I'd done many forms of illegal substances years ago, and this always disgusted me when I looked back over those foolish escapades.

Later on that evening, I checked on Anna - a peaceful sleep caused by the medication made her lay restful on the couch, so I put a yellow patterned blanket over her and gave her a couple of duck feather pillows so she could support her head. After picking up some tufts of carpet and more broken ornaments lying on the room's floor, caused by Rex going berserk due to the commotion earlier, I picked up the green bottle of French brandy from the drinks' cupboard, then shut the living room door quietly.

Rex sat in the kitchen, his new habitat for tonight, and I stroked him to help the dog settle down peacefully this late evening.

After a couple of hours and to my shame I'd drunk about half a bottle of brandy while sitting in the bedroom. The events over the last few days and weeks had affected my reasoning. I was full of fear and rage about what must be happening. The drinking I *knew* would not help the problem but yet I continued. I began punching the bed in frustration; drunkenness and anger reinforced by the consumption of added glasses of brandy overwhelmed me. The radio played 'memory laden tunes' of times gone by, and sadly, even in spite of these tunes, I could not relax and remain composed. I got up from the bed and wandered out carrying the half empty bottle of brandy.

I went to the landing window unsteadily where Anna encountered this ghost and I gazed out, it seemed dark and quiet outside with only the silver shine of the moon lighting the star filled sky. Something did not feel right though; I pressed my face up against the window in despair when suddenly *I* felt an icy breeze brush by the side of me. I gritted my teeth for I knew this presence must be *back* in the house.

Angrily I yelled with fury. 'You Bastard! You are still here.'

Infuriated and with all my inhibitions vanishing I ran downstairs to switch the master electric button on that controlled the power to the workshop. I snatched the keys and rushed upstairs unlocking the workshop door before entering. I turned the lights and everything else on including the infamous Diode machine.

I was now incensed. 'Right!' I yelled. 'Speak to me. I demand a response Natasha?' I put my hands on the desk and leaned forward. In a demanding tone I persisted. 'Do you wish to say something you piece of shit or whatever you are?' This sentence I pronounced achieved nothing. I asked again more forcefully.

'Natasha! Answer me! Now!'

The Diode machine indicators flickered and then Natasha's

'voice' came through in a hissing robotic slow manner.

'A ghost in your tape machine. A ghost in your phone!'

I dropped the brandy bottle that my sweaty hand had been clutching onto the floor. I took a few steps back and asked another question.

'Who scared Anna today?' A delay followed for a few seconds.

'Stan came to *your* house!' Natasha replied mechanically.

I paced up and down and faced away from the Diode machine. 'Stan, or whoever is mimicking him would never frighten me or my wife in this obscene way.' My emotions were livid, and hastily I revolved clockwise and pointed my eyes to give a bullish stare.

'Believe Andrew!' Natasha's voice was phonetic: 'We are in your house. *I walk in the mirror of your desires.*'

A male voice came through hissing an unearthly laugh before it spoke: 'Stan is here. I live. I am not dead.'

An idea then came into my mind. The old man had made a 'promise to me' in his life that when he died he would give an answer to a specific question, confirming his spirit had *survived* in some form after death. I tore back into my bedroom and after pulling most of my personal documents out of a small filing case; I finally found an envelope. This contained the scrap of paper written twenty years earlier. I opened it and I read the phrase scrawled in blue ink. *Time is the Essence. For the rest of my Duties* were the words written down. This phrase, how vaguely insignificant at the time, was evidential, and if repeated would prove without a shadow of doubt that Stan could have survived in some form after physical death. I put the paper in my pocket and walked back into the workshop. I subsequently put a question to the Stan personality.

'If you are Stan, what is the phrase of *words* you told me when you were alive, which would prove to me your personality, or spirit has remained intact after your physical death.' There was silence and just the eerie sound of 'whispering voices' and other noisy radio interference. I banged my hand down hard in front of the Diode machine and angrily demanded:

'Answer me. ANSWER! You goddamn son of a bitch!'

Natasha struck back with a response. 'We can shout! From the "City of the Dead."'

'You've still not answered my question,' I raged.

The ghost, impersonating Stan, countered in a slow pronounced manner. 'Dreams come through the soul.'

I shook my head in condemnation. 'You are wrong. I have it written down what the original Stan told me. So if you will excuse me from your sick and twisted game...' I was interrupted by another disturbing quotation from this 'Stan Personality.'

'Two men you hated are now dead. For murder is all around you. You wanted them scoundrels dead Andrew. And I...I did your bidding!'

'What do you mean,' I replied agitated. Silence greeted me for a minute - so I made another point to this would be antagonist.

'I do not believe your lies anymore, it's over. Whoever you are I denounce your reality! You are all myths and you disgust me with your lies.' I grabbed the brandy bottle off the floor and 'screamed' for these experiments to all 'end.'

'You cannot just switch us off Andrew,' Natasha asserted with fury. 'You are nothing but an ignorant human being. Who do you think you are dealing with? The link is becoming stronger. I will soon be able to manifest into your world and destroy you. Do you understand me Andrew? Someone else is already stalking your house ready to finish your beloved Anna.'

'Natasha!' I angrily retorted. 'Don't make idle threats against my wife or me, you have no power to harm anyone.' The room then started to vibrate. I glanced around and all of my electronic devices were coming on and off including the lights. There was then an awful loud 'demonic groan' and hiss that bellowed the words:

'TAKE ADVICE FROM THE ELECTRONIC GHOSTS OF THE DEAD... ANDREW STEIN!'

I completely lost control of myself and threw the brandy bottle against the wall. It smashed into pieces sending fragments of green glass flying everywhere. I grabbed the Diode machine in anger but before I could do anything I felt a massive burst of electric power pass through my body. My muscles went into spasms and convulsions. My arms felt terrible pain. Somehow I managed with all my strength to pull the mighty Diode machine off the desk and onto the floor with a crash. I fell down dazed and looked around. The fax machine then made some beeping noises and a piece of paper came out. I struggled up and tore the fax out of the machine. My eyes were shocked to see the blurred dark face of a woman on it and the words: *You will die Stein, from your friend Natasha.* I stared in shocked disbelief. The tape machine reels began spinning anticlockwise and the walls of the workshop were making scratching noises.

Suddenly all the lights went off in the room and I felt an invisible force push me to the ground. The door to the workshop was trying to close but luckily splinters of glass from the brandy bottle had wedged underneath the door keeping it from shutting. I felt an electrical charge scratch my face. I tried desperately to get out; I then felt something jump onto my back. It felt like an animal. I yelled for whatever it might be to 'get off.' I gazed behind me for a moment before I moved my head back around to the front. Something happened next that did indeed bring a dreadful fear into my mind. Directly ahead of me a blue orange like mist was beginning to form into a shape, it illuminated part of the darkened workshop. Unbelieving of what I saw, I surely felt it must be the drink. It certainly wasn't though. In a flash an apparition of a *cat* appeared only half a metre away from my face, the haunting vision of 'Tiger' crouched before me, fully materialized disturbing my brain further. The door seemed destined to finally close shut. I managed to scramble off the floor somehow and found my torch lying on the desk; it usually hung on the wall near where the Diode machine used to stand. I switched the torch's beam onto where this ghost cat crouched. The cat let out a dreadful animal sound; *its* eyes became large and turned a pale red before it jumped up at me lashing out with its grey decomposing paws, they scratched painfully into my arms. My hands grappled with this creature as the curtains in the workshop were pulled from the windows and a number of my tools were thrown in my direction. I shouted loudly - then all of a sudden this cat apparition vanished. I managed to put my arm onto the moving workshop door to stop it and regain my tentative balance. A screwdriver flew through the air and hit the door just missing my head.

I ran out of the workshop, went downstairs to the fuse box near the damaged front door and clearly knew the electricity had to be cut off to the room. I pressed the button to eliminate the power. My hand convulsed as I touched the switch - this caused one of the main fuses to short-circuit.

In my panicked state I could hear other objects continuously being thrown against the wall of the workshop upstairs for a further fifteen minutes, before silence ended the disturbances. Breathing with relief my back slid down the wall by the fuse box to the floor. I sat there in deep regretful thought for a long time, my head sank into my hands and I sobbed in despair until I descended into a turbulent troublesome sleep due to exhaustion.

Chapter 10

Dr. Hans Neily Investigates

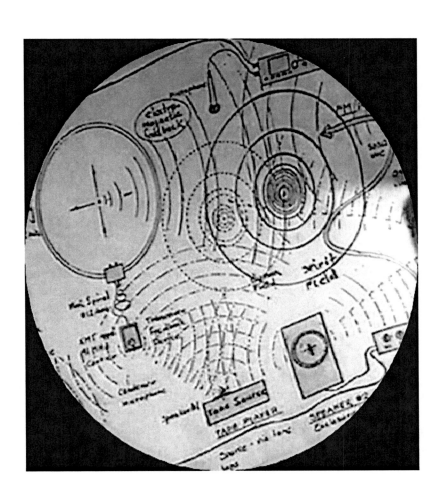

Four days went by from the unexplained incidents involving Anna and myself. I relayed the disturbing events to Michael and he fully understood my predicament. Therefore Michael, to my relief - got in touch with someone who had bountiful knowledge in this field of strange and scientific phenomena. This man's name was 'Dr. Hans Neily', a lecturer in some large institute of paranormal research. His parents were half-German and half-English, confusing his bloodline nationally. He bore the stature of a very tall well built man in the latter stages of middle age. A beard covered part of his face and brown slicked back hair was brushed neatly off his brow. Hans Neily decided after much 'persuasion' to come round to my chaotic house to investigate and evaluate the incidents taking place.

Michael accompanied him to the outside of our boarded up front door. The late afternoon sunshine reflected onto Hans' spectacles causing him to remove them and unbutton his chequered tweed jacket. This large man's expertise in many aspects of science always filled him with benign confidence before any case he was called to assess. He *gazed* up and down at our red brick house and around the driveway path curiously. A large black shoulder bag hung heavily on his shoulder containing electronic devices he used to aid him in his ghostly work. Hans knocked on our house door firmly. Sitting with Anna in the living room the arrival of this man, I have to admit - made our feelings become fraught with dreadful nerves - nearly rendering us speechless. These contributed to create giant butterflies in our stomachs due to the arrival of this yet unknown guest. I wearily rose up from the couch and consoled Anna in a reassuring manner.

'That'll be Michael with his companion, Dr. Neily. I will civilly invite these people in.' After a 'brief greeting' I asked them both into our house. Anna could hear my voice talking with Michael and this man's. She took a deep breath and tried to act calm, this was surely an achievement - because of the happenings that had upset her over the last few weeks. Dr. Hans Neily entered the living room and put on his large spectacles. He assumed the presence of an *Orson Welles'* character.

'You must be Dr. Neily. Thank you for coming,' said Anna nervously. Dr. Neily took off his black bag from his large shoulder and placed it on the floor, he gave a slight smile towards Anna and told her to just call him by the name Hans.

'Would you like something to drink Dr. Neily, sorry I meant Hans?' asked Anna.

He rubbed his hands together in a strong and confident manner. 'I could sure do with a double whisky. It helps my concentration you see Mrs. Stein.' He then let out a slight chuckle. Anna agreed to the request while telling Michael and myself not to worry and to sit down, as she would prepare us all a stiff alcoholic beverage. Dr. Hans Neily asked Michael to pass him some technical papers and he began reading in a refined manner for a few moments.

'Before I have my drink Mr. Stein,' said Hans in an articulate way. 'I want to visit the place in this house where you have been conducting your electronic experiments.'

'If you insist Hans. By the way just call me Andrew, we're on first name terms now,' I replied. We chatted for another minute when Anna told everyone that she had to pop next door for an hour to talk with Carol. Anna left the room before I made my way to the hallway.

I beckoned Hans to follow me, and he picked up his black bag and did as he was told. I stepped upstairs and glanced behind *at* Hans, who followed in measured succession, I think his weight was beginning to affect him as I heard a few heavy breaths coming from his oversized chest. We continued until we reached the outside of the workshop door and then said a few comments to each other.

'The trouble has been brewing for the last month,' I said. 'But it came to a head. And became totally uncontrollable a few days ago. It all began when Tiger our cat went berserk while in my workshop for no rational reason.'

'Rational!' replied Hans. 'Wait Andrew. *Cats* are very sensitive to anything spiritual or paranormal, it would not go berserk for no reason.'

'Interesting observation, well anyway the cat's dead now, run—'

Hans interrupted me. 'Please Andrew I already know. There is no need to repeat the usual sob-story to me.'

I became irritated at his ill-mannered behaviour - but did not let it bother me so I continued. 'If I can say, a couple of nights ago everything went crazy. My wife Anna saw something at the landing stairs window. Then I began to sense something alien might be in the workshop with *me*. I was attacked by something I cannot explain.'

'I recognize your worries Andrew. I've been reading the "report" you gave to Michael documenting the Diode machine and spirit voices you have been communicating with.'

I winked at Hans. Then with some uncertainty I slowly unlocked the workshop door and pushed it open making it bang on the wall.

Hans entered into the room and began observing the different instruments and equipment that lay scattered about. The item that *grabbed* this man's attention was the enormous reddish brown metal encased 'Diode machine' I'd constructed. It looked like something out of a science fiction movie; it still rested on the floor from where I had pulled it off the desk the other night. Hans put his black bag on one of the workshops few intact shelves. He opened the bag then removed one of his strange electronic devices from within it. After completing this necessary chore Hans made his electronic instrument function, it made a few circumspect bleeps and crackling sounds. He took it upon himself to make some careful adjustments and observed my broken Diode machine again. Hans stared at me with a stern expression.

'So this is the troublesome machine you built to make two-way conversation possible with an unknown force.'

'That's correct,' I replied.

'You know, no one was ever able to achieve this - except *William O Neil* and *George W Meek*…I have heard the tapes Michael gave me to listen and experiment on. The voice of *Natasha* and the voice of this *Stan personality* were some of the most impressive I have ever heard during my tireless research.'

I felt quite proud of his comments he made about my results obtained from the Diode machine I'd built. But I could not let this compliment distract attention away from the whole nightmare episode hanging over my wife and me. I wanted this whole paranormal experiment, foolishly commenced by me to end.

Hans with some difficulty lifted my Diode machine over onto its side and put his electronic, or whatever he used to aid him with this work - over it. Hans' electronic device then went crazy.

'What's that you have in your possession?' I remarked. 'And what does it do.'

'In scientific terms this is my, well you could call it my electronic eyes and ears. If there is something in this workshop my instrument will detect it. Now Andrew, close the door and wait outside.'

'Is that a wise thing to undertake. You know the situation?'

'You heard what I said. Without delay do it Andrew.'

I did what Hans asked me and shut the workshop door gradually to a close. Hans cautiously checked around turning his head to the side for a brief moment and listened. He saw the overturned reel-to-reel tape recorder and noticed the lumps of broken glass from the brandy bottle and other tools littering the concrete floor. He again observed the 'Diode machine' that I'd made. Suddenly his electronic instrument started reacting with out of control readings. Hans glanced around and then felt a slight icy whoosh sensation rub past him.

I tapped on the door to see if he was okay in there. He abruptly shouted: 'Don't disturb me! Everything is normal.'

Hans with agitation - grabbed - and then examined the recorder and tried to remove the big reel of magnetic tape from it. His hand only touched the recorder for a few moments when he felt an electric charge race up his arm, he cried out in pain. Then his electronic instrument shot away from his other hand's grasp. It dropped to the ground in a gradual slow motion before moving about on the floor on its own accord. Then like a cascading thunderbolt pushing its direction, it flew backwards smashing against the back wall with some force. The Diode machine began making sounds that formed into a strange 'electrical humming' sound. Hans heard quite clearly the words: *Natasha Is Here.*

Because there was no power going into the machine this helped him make an assessment of what mysterious phenomena he was dealing with.

My curious impatience with this stranger nosing about in my workshop caused me rudely to reopen the workshop door, very much to the annoyance of Hans Neily. Subsequently I put my thoughts and opinions to him frankly.

'Listen,' I said. 'I want to know what is going on in here. This is my house, not some kind of Edwardian freak show.'

Hans was about to reply when his large arm began to shake and move without him having any control. Then suddenly his large right hand took a hold of my dark green shirt and tried to force me to the floor.

'What the hell are you doing? I snapped. 'Take your hand off me!'

'I can't!' said Hans. 'I can't control my bodily functions. There is something attacking me.' Hans' shaky balance then caused him to stumble on a large hammer lying on the floor.

'If this is a German joke, it isn't funny. Now pull yourself together, man!' If there were any humorous notions hanging over me - they evaporated when a dull thud impacted onto the large man. He'd been punched in the back by something unseen.

'I've been goddamn hit!' barked Hans. 'Does that sound like a joke? I'm not playing around here! Break the link Andrew. Whatever it is - it is using *you* for *its* power.'

I experienced at first hand what he meant when an invisible hand slapped me hard across the face accompanied by a loud pop in my left eardrum, then poltergeist activity occurred and the Diode machine began rocking from side to side. I shouted for Michael to 'come upstairs to help us both.' After what seemed an eternity Michael came to our assistance and managed to release the large man's grip from my shirt.

'Out now! Leave!' demanded Hans, as he lifted his damaged electronic device off the floor. The three of us managed to escape from whatever inhabited the workshop and I slammed the door shut. A large object impacted against the door from the interior demonstrating something was alive in my workshop.

'There should be no activity in there,' challenged Hans. 'You said you cut the power!'

'The power is off,' I declared. I turned to Michael and told him to go downstairs and wait for Anna to come back from next door, which he did. The large man and me were the only ones left standing on the stairs landing. Hans filled his oversized chest with a deep breath and paced slowly, soldier like around. I straightened my shirt awkwardly and I was inquisitive with my question.

'Did you sense anything? And conversely, and most importantly: Did you *see* anything?'

Hans stopped and remained still for a moment. 'Yes! You have certainly got something in here.' He let out a nervous chuckle. 'Definitely, no doubt about it! I've experienced other phenomena before. But never with this much power in the daytime, normally it's at the height of the night time you might achieve this kind of direct psychokinesis.' He stared intently at the readings his electronic device had recorded before it got broken by this unseen force one last time, and asked me to go downstairs into the living room, as he would follow shortly.

Thirty minutes later myself, Anna and Michael were sitting down in the lounge taking a few sips from our drinks when Hans entered without saying anything. He gulped down the rest of his whisky - placing the glass on the coffee table. I felt somewhat guilty and tried to be pleasant and hospitable: 'For what it's worth. You can have another drink,' I said. 'I don't blame you! After what's taken place so far.'

'No, I've had enough for the time being,' he replied. He moved to the centre of the room as if he was a divine guru and cleared his throat. 'Everybody, I have to talk to you all now.' We all put down our glasses and became attentive, like children taking a first geometry lesson might act. We had no idea what to expect.

'Where is your dog?' asked Hans.

'Our dog Rex is round my sister's for the time being,' answered Anna downcast. 'We thought it best for him to be out of the way.' Hans' facial features became serious, and with his large presence filling us all with expectation - we waited to hear what this person would speak about next.

'The situation with your unfortunate experiences, plus other strange incidents told to me by Michael. Including the voices, which I heard on the tape you have made Andrew, have led me to this conclusion.'

'What is that?' I asked intrigued.

'Electronic Voice Phenomena and Spiricom, a professional building of a machine to contact the dead from another dimension is a science in its own right. Dismissed by many psychics, mediums and people in religion as dabbling with an Electronic occult. It is a proven method. Or you could say a way of penetrating the place where some of the departed souls of people who once lived on this Earth now reside.' Hans' words were spoken with authority - and he had the persona of a university scholar about him.

Michael smiled with some amusement at this lecture by Hans; Michael was the most skeptical about these metaphors being preached. Hans turned to Michael and an irritated expression was etched on his face. 'Something amusing you. You think you're better practised?'

I stared at Michael with daggers so he got the message on how I felt about his mocking attitude. Michael's expression dropped and he made his excuses before telling Hans 'he was thinking about something else that he found funny.' The big man regained his composure and continued. 'There is a number of experimenters around the world who have been involved in this subject, and have received amazing results. The institute in Switzerland called

IBNT has now started to use Videocom.'

Interested I leaned forward in my chair and asked:

'What is Videocom?'

'It is a way with video cameras and televisions tuned to a channel that is not receiving a broadcast signal, to obtain pictures and other images from the "other side" called the Astral Timestream. The Astral Timestream is a spirit technician's station. Furthermore, due to this incredible discovery, some qualified experimenters have been able to make contact and record deceased people onto *Videotape*. Many prominent historical figures have appeared, including *Jules Verne, H.G. Wells*, plus other researchers who have been involved in this subject. Like *Konstantin Raudive* and *Frederick Jurgheson*, two of the main scientists involved in initiating this unexplained science.' Hans then got some pictures out of his bag and passed them to all of us to decide what we thought.

The pictures were truly amazing, though certain things puzzled me. If these prominent people who'd died in the early 1900s were now making contact, why are the clothes they seemed to be wearing in these spirit pictures encompassing typical 1980s' suits, including the thin black leather tie. Michael made this point to Hans - but he came back with some answer saying they were doing this to make them 'acceptable' and more in tune with the times we were all living in now. I must admit I found Dr. Neily's answers awkwardly evasive of believable facts - but I kept my own negative prejudices to myself. Anna then asked our intellectual guest a question, hesitantly.

'So...I have looked at these pictures...and heard what you have been saying. But what has all this got to do with these circumstances happening to me? And the events of destruction going on in Andrew's workshop?'

'I will tell you Anna,' said Hans. 'You can say that it takes all sorts to make a world. There are comedians, the jokers, and the most treacherous of all - are the ones who want to shamefully cause a disturbance in one's *mind*, a psychological attack to be precise. This applies on the other side of life, or spirit world as it is generally referred to in psychic circles. To be more specific it is like this.' Hans took a few extra steps around the room as if he was a resilient politician and continued.

'There are seven heavens in the world beyond, transitions or levels of mind where certain people go. Most people when they die wake up and find themselves in the second heaven. It is a sort of resting place where people adjust and learn before they can go to the next heaven plane. These people have come through to researchers in this world, and have given intelligent and informative advice about the place where they now inhabit.' He pondered for a moment of reflection then recommenced another sentence. 'Now that does not concern us in your case.'

'Then what do you mean?' I asked.

'What I mean Andrew is that we are dealing here with the first heaven, or the lower astral plane as it is sometimes called. It is a kind of living hell world of purgatory and regret. Here you will find criminals. Sex perverts, also confused or materially obsessed individuals who are desperate to have their material things with them, but cannot gain access to these precious commodities anymore. The more evil a person is, then the more they will attract to themselves entities of a similar nature to their misguided surroundings. This part of the astral plane is closest to our earth, and is thus easier for them to communicate with us...I have heard the recordings you have made of the robotic sounding voices and in my own judgment some form of contact has been established between you, Andrew - and these malevolent entities.'

I wanted to put my own spin on this. 'I cant be sure, of what you are implicating. It specifically states in the books I have read about this subject, that these ghosts or entities as you refer to have to come from a spirit transmission station on the other side, and cannot come from any other source.'

'Listen Andrew,' Hans told me. 'If someone is inexperienced in the procedure of these experiments they are undertaking, they can contact a destructive force from the lower astral plane, which will use all its devious ploys to suck the investigator into making conversations with it. It will gain power from the emotions of fear, rage, and deceit. So markedly, and eventually, it will find a way to break free from its morbid existence and attack the experimenter for its own perverse gratification. I dealt with a case in France where a man was basically sent out of his mind by hearing non-human voices, not from the tapes he had made, but from inside his own head. The symptoms resembled "paranoid schizophrenia." Now tell me Andrew, when you were talking to the Stan personality, what did you feel about him, and the comments he made?'

I thought for a moment then answered. 'That it definitely cannot be the Stan who I once knew.'

Hans asked me a more intense question. 'Now this is very important. What did you feel about the Natasha personality, remember this is the entity or ghost if you call it that, which firstly, and most importantly, initiated the two-way conversation with the aid of your Diode machine?'

'Well without a shadow of a doubt that it was sinister,' I replied nervously.

'Then your feelings serve you justice Andrew. Because your instinct cannot be deceived,' he remarked.

I looked at Anna briefly, then at Hans. 'What about the image of this Stan personality my wife claims she witnessed up against the landing window?'

'In my opinion, and by what Anna told me about the incident—' Hans paused before giving the dramatic reply I personally dreaded. 'An earthbound demon, which has found a way to manifest into this world with the aid of your Diode machine.' This reply affected Anna with acute fear and a few tears trickled down her cheeks to relieve the stress.

I myself became unnerved by these comments I'd listened to. I found it hard to take *in* what this paranormal scientist was describing. It seemed like something out of a 'Hammer Horror Movie'. Nevertheless I could not ignore the facts of my own eyes. With all my previous disbeliefs about ghosts and life after death niggling at me, I knew that rational or sane explanations to dismiss the paranormal subjects of 'Electronic Voice Phenomena' and 'Spiricom' was no longer sustainable. The disturbing events of the last few weeks had proved my undoing. For emphatically, there is some other kind of cosmic sphere where the dead souls of people, and other non-human creatures reside in. Dr. Neily's scientific sermon put paid to anymore skeptical notions. I just wondered what the large man might articulate further.

Hans Neily's brow furrowed and he stood tall.

'Now! It is up to me and Andrew to banish this force! Banish it back from where it has come. I want you Michael to go to my van outside and bring in my video cameras, and the main TV monitor, then to mount the cameras up along the stairs. Wait for me to give you further instructions about what other equipment I may need.' Michael still seemed slightly skeptical, and had doubts about what might be going on in Hans Neily's head. Either he was a renowned investigator into this paranormal science, or he had the mind of a mad man.

'Excuse me!' huffed Michael. 'You're getting ahead of yourself, aren't you. Who do you think you are? An Electronic Exorcist!' This seemed to anger Hans and he hit back instantly with his curtailing disapproval. 'Don't make stupid comments! This is stuff you definitely do not fool about with.' These words were exclaimed brutally in his non-descript German accent. I intervened to try and calm things down before telling Michael to do what he was asked, which after a bit of prostration he did. Michael went outside to get the equipment.

Next I turned to Anna. 'I suggest, you've been through enough over the last few days. Why don't you go back and stay with your sister Janice, and remain there for the time being. Until we try and sort this ghostly episode out.'

'No!' shot Anna.

'Okay then. What about John and Carol, our next-door neighbours.'

'You don't listen. No I will not.' Then in a courageous tone Anna reiterated her stubbornness. 'This is my house, and I'm not going to let it get ripped apart by you lot. Anyway, I've seen this thing that terrified me once. I'm not going to let it frighten me again. I'm staying here with you Andrew.' She instantly held my hand gently.

'Anna I'm worried about what will happen.'

She was just about to have a row with me when I intervened with a 'diplomatic quotation' as I didn't want to embarrass our guest Dr. Neily. I further cooled the situation by telling her that she 'certainly had guts to not want to run away,' especially after the events she'd witnessed.

I faced back around to Hans. 'What can I do. A wife is a wife. She wants to stay here.'

Hans sighed and had a pained expression; he mumbled a few words that sounded German, paused for a moment, looked at his gold-strapped watch before giving a concise reply. 'So be it then.' Next his face went stern: 'Will you excuse me, Andrew. Things to do I'm afraid.' He then left the room to help Michael get the various electronic equipment from the van parked outside.

After he went, for some reason the small blue painted *China*

Doll, resting on the cream coloured ornate fireplace and given to me by the long dead Stan caught *my* vision. It was one of only a few ornaments that survived due to reckless damage caused by our once distressed pets. I wondered with weary intuitions if it, or any of us would come out unscathed.

Chapter 11

Encounters with the Unknown

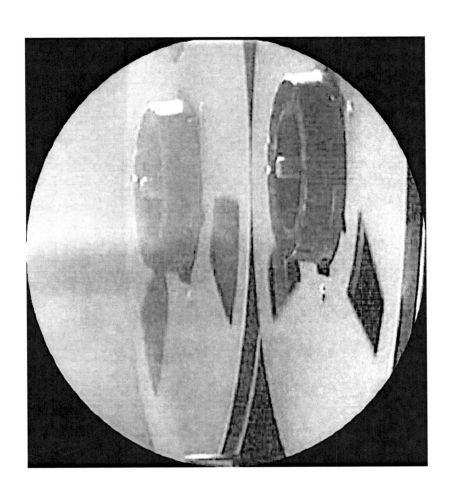

The time on the clock hanging high up on the light yellow painted hallway pointed to 9.00p.m. - we were in the midst of mid-evening. Michael had set up and positioned a few video cameras on the wall leading up the stairs. One camera was fixed with sturdy brackets on the landing at the top of the staircase, and one on the wall opposite my paranormal infested workshop. Two television sets were being used as monitors downstairs in the hallway, with other numerous electronic indicators and devices. They all were resting on a make shift table that Hans had made.

A big reel-to-reel tape recorder, like the one in my workshop accompanied a couple of radios, plus an electronic temperature graph-reader was bleeping - so consequently, this completed the assortment of electrical equipment. Everything was nearly set up to Hans' requirements. Michael was in the process of making some final adjustments to one of the video cameras situated on the staircase wall. He 'shouted' downwards in the direction of Hans, whose *eyes* were staring anxiously at the electronic monstrosities he owned. Another Diode machine made by a fellow colleague at the University where he lectured was placed precisely on the middle of the table. Hans told me he'd never obtained the results I'd achieved with my own machine. Thus for that reason, and whatever morbid fascination was inside his mind,

Dr. Neily had decided to see if he might be able to obtain a direct two-way conversation with a suchlike entity or ghost that seemed to be causing the trouble in my house.

'I've made the connections Hans, are you getting any pictures on the TVs?' inquired Michael. The big man who'd begun to sweat bent down slightly and studied the television picture closely, he sat down on a chair and made a few adjustments. The buttons for the brightness and contrast were turned clockwise and Hans could see Michael's face on the camera he'd meticulously fitted. With an enthusiastic expression on his face and in a loud voice he yelled:

'Yes! Perfectly done Michael. You're not as stupid as you make out. Even in spite of reckless interpretations - you sometimes make!' Hans then asked Anna and me to come out from the kitchen for a moment.

I put my coffee cup down and slowly stepped out of the dish-laden kitchen with Anna following cautiously behind me. I stood by the side of Hans before peering hard at the television monitors. I must admit I *felt* a touch of excitement, which I know must seem absurd, but the whole set up had been done very professionally by Hans Neily and Michael.

'What's up Hans? I asked in an inquisitive voice. 'Why all these video cameras positioned up along the stairs?'

Anna remained further back from the big man and myself. I think the video cameras gave her a sense of unease. Especially because of the damage they had inflicted onto the walls, what with the various holding brackets and chipped plaster - all done to secure the cameras in pointed positions.

I spoke a few 'metaphysical sentences' while Hans moved in accordance of importance the electronic gadgets neatly laid all along the makeshift table. After my short conversation with him I beckoned my wife to come closer, which eventually she did. Hans moved his enormous backside around on his chair in some kind of discomfort, I'm sure he must have been suffering from haemorrhoids or piles as they are known to everyone, but I did not dare ask him. He looked at me with serious eyes before speaking. 'Andrew, everything is set up and prepared for this procedure...We are going to undertake one hell of an experiment. There will be no time for jokes. You are to act precisely, in the way that I see fit.'

'Okay. Name what I am supposed we do?' I replied. 'Remember, I've never worked with someone - with your so-called scientific pedigree before.'

Hans faced back towards the televisions and commented: 'When Michael has finished positioning the final camera. I want you to reconnect the power to your workshop.'

I was hesitant and unsure for a moment. 'Is that wise?'

'Just do what I say. I know what I'm doing.'

Michael ran back down the stairs brushing past Anna and myself before kneeling by the side of Dr. Neily. Michael observed the television picture on the monitors and seemed quite proud of his achievement of being able to get the electronic stuff to function. 'Not a bad job, hey. I have no idea what you are expecting to appear, but whatever it is...human or paranormal, these video cameras and recorders will pick it up. We might even get Harry Houdini, or King Henry The VIII make an appearance.' Michael then guffawed.

'Don't be a fool!' remarked Hans with displeasure. 'This is not some game you idiot.'

This turn of phrase angered Michael after the hard work he'd just completed and he showed his disapproval with venomous undertones. 'That's great! Thank you. Thanks a bloody lot. I take offence easily. If it weren't for me pal, you'd never have known about Andrew's ghostly experiments. Ungrateful German sod!'

Hans was just about to get up - and by the expression on his face land a right hook on my friend - so quickly I intervened.

'Come on for God's sake! This is no time to be fighting amongst ourselves. Michael, stop being flippant! What is it with you?' Michael had been about to speak some other 'rude comment' when I gave him a stern stare. Subsequently, and after a tentative moment, Michael's brazenness died down.

'Alright,' he said. 'I get the picture. Remember though, I'm not doing this to take insults after working my bollocks off.'

My reasoning suggested there was some kind of rivalry between Hans Neily and Michael. But I had no idea from what past experience *it* stemmed from. Hans huffed with indifference - while flicking a few switches on his silver coloured control panel, this action showed the picture each camera would record. He instructed Michael, after an awkward pause, to check the video machines were connected correctly.

Anna stepped slightly closer for a better view. Michael stood up and moved to the right where the video machines were situated; he next carried out the order given by the big man. 'Everything is working correctly and I can see no problems,' stated Michael strongly.

Hans pointed his finger in my direction and told me to 'reconnect the power to my workshop.' I must say I was slightly nervous, but agreed that I would do as he asked. I slowly went to the fuse box situated under the stairs while carefully avoiding the numerous wires lying untidily around on the floor. I waited for a second and gave Hans another *glance*.

'Do as I demand,' exclaimed Hans. 'Press down on the switch.'

I put my left hand onto the fuse box and took a deep breath. Suddenly there was a blue spark of light and I felt a sharp shock, this caused my nervous body to jolt backwards. 'Shit! What the hell is that!' Anna came to my aid and asked if I was hurt. I told her I felt slightly shaken but otherwise okay. I turned to Hans. 'Why did you make me do that for?' You know! Why! I explained to you earlier there is no wretched power feeding up to my workshop.'

'Mr. Stein, do not question my motives. I am aware of what is going on.' Hans' face then became focused.

I composed myself and asked him 'what were we to do now.' He just made a short comment of 'Wait and be patient man,' before he got up from his seat and went to view one of the video cameras on the stair wall.

A couple of hours later and everything seemed quiet. Michael sat in the living room talking Clairvoyance subjects with Anna - which seemed peculiar, but I myself needed a more personal chat with this Dr. Hans Neily. I wanted to know exactly what he'd done in the past to connect him to this ghostly scientific phenomenon. I gradually approached him and had a questioning look on my face.

'You don't mind me inquiring, but can you tell me what's your background in the paranormal, and the sciences of Electronic Voice Phenomena and Spiricom?'

Hans moved his face up from the *Psychic Magazine* he was reading and addressed me in an intellectual manner. 'Andrew if you must know, I was once part of a panel of electrical experts who tested Konstantin Raudive on his spirit voices he captured, along with the tapes he used in his recording methods. We conducted many tests to see if they might be fraudulent. The investigators of German psychic research, GPR desperately wanted this. But the scientist confounded all the critics, including myself, and we had no alternative to accept as fact - the results Raudive made. That is what got me involved in this part of paranormal research, but it's not the only unusual subject which caused a rapturous fascination to fill my brain. When I was young, my mother, who practiced as a Spiritualist medium, began inviting friends to the many séances she instigated to contact the deceased.

I watched many strange events happening. But at one sitting which I was allowed to attend on my fourteenth birthday, my mother went into a trance and a Spirit, or ghost, call it what you will, came into her and spoke.'

'What did it say?' I asked enthralled.

'I won't go into complete detail, but the "spirit" claimed to be from one person of the expedition party that British explorer Colonel Percy Fawcett took into the jungles of South America.'

'Wait a minute!' I commented. 'I read about Percy Fawcett. He was the explorer who travelled into the Amazon jungle in the 1920s to find a lost city of unknown riches and people. Killed by native tribal Indians the book stated.'

'You're correct Andrew and this always intrigued me, I suppose this is what got me interested at such a young age with the ludicrous idea of wanting to find out what really happened to him, and the other poor souls who accompanied the Colonel. When my mother died I inherited a small fortune, and after reading many books about *Colonel Percy Fawcett*, I became so obsessed with the *Fawcett* expedition, that I arranged my own in 1964 to see if I could find how he died. Our adventure though, was ill planned and beset by problems as soon as we arrived in Bolivia. What with the heat and the disease, which cut down half of my expeditionary force. The rest of us encountered hostile "Amazonian Indians" further into the forest past the "Dead Horse" encampment, the place written about by the Colonel in his diary before he vanished. The situation deteriorated, and cost one man to lose his life when the Indians stole most of our equipment. My dear friend Professor Wolfgang Peterson tried to persuade our antagonists to return what they had stolen - but during some confusion he was speared in the stomach. I witnessed his pleading face and I tried to get to him to save his life, but the arrows and sticks thrown at me by these fierce indigenous people beat me back. Professor Wolfgang then got speared in the neck, which killed him instantly; his body was lifted away into the jungle, held aloft in triumph by the Indians. My help to him had been futile. My remaining colleagues in the party screamed at me that all of us had to run for our lives, as we would surely end up the same way as my friend. We were forced to abandon the whole nauseating adventure. This not only disappointed me greatly, especially the death of a close friend, but I had also used up most of the money left to me in my inheritance to fund it. I was ridiculed in the German press for my antics and faced a lawsuit from the widow of Professor Wolfgang Peterson, which in the end left me penniless, to further add to my humiliation, fellow academics and scientists briefed against me, making outlandish accusations. These peoples' despicable lies eventually forced me out of Germany. I went to the USA for a time before eventually coming to England.' Hans sighed deeply and his head bowed to the floor for a moment. I could see this had been a traumatic event for him and I felt some profound sympathy. The man regained his *Orson Welles'* presence and continued.

'It taught me one thing though. Do not take the advice from any spirit or entity. My ill-fated Fawcett escapade proved that. The advice from any "spiritualist medium" must be treated skeptically, that also applies to other means like the electronic methods you have used. Be objective, but be cautious. That is my experience, and I have witnessed many cases of paranormal activity.'

I was fascinated by what this big man had told me; he obviously must have encountered many intriguing events. We talked a few minutes longer - then Michael came out from the living room and asked Hans if he wanted anything else to be checked.

Later on, time passed by slowly for me due to my various ghostly conversations. Then in between fleeting glances in the living room - I noticed the clock on the wall displayed 1.00 a.m. 'Time is a strange tool,' I thought. 'It works in mysterious ways. I wonder if the dead are aware of its ticking presence.'

In the hallway Michael 'chatted quietly to Hans,' and next began the process of helping the big man make important adjustments. Buttons and wires were fixed with a screwdriver and a hammer, and then they both observed the electronic readings.

'Interesting. Interesting,' murmured Hans. He grabbed a pen and quickly noted down the temperature from the large thermometer

I myself rested in the living room and felt light-headed. Anna had dozed off to sleep and we were sitting up against each other like a couple of museum exhibits on the sofa. Only a few other house lights were left on.

In the hallway Michael poked Hans in the arm. 'I'm going outside to have a cigarette. Do you mind?'

'Go on then and be quick about it!' Hans' irate eyes subsequently followed Michael to the door.

Michael stepped outside of the house and slowly took a few paces onto the damp grass. He glanced around before taking out a packet of his camel cigarettes; he removed one of them slowly from the packet then lit it. Michael made sure he took a deep puff from this white and brown tobacco stick. The wind now started to pick up and the trees across the road began to sway in different directions. The nocturnal wildlife sounds he could hear seemed to increase in volume and a fox darted across the road as if it has been disturbed by *something*. It stopped for a second, watching Michael, before it ran away into the thick undergrowth across the road. Michael whistled and walked a few steps further from the house.

In the living room I was drifting in and out of sleep, but I must admit I found it impossible to relax, Anna continued to sleep though. My eyes flickered open and I stretched a few muscles taking care not to disturb my wife, who rested gently against my shoulder. For some reason I began to feel uneasy as if *I* was being observed by *something* - I felt fearful for I knew that something was about to happen, I just hoped it would not be my unfortunate self to experience it.

Back outside Michael had finished his cigarette. He ground the smoking butt with his shoe into the soil and prepared to go back into the house. At that moment Michael's attention was grabbed and he saw what seemed to be an old man moving past him along the road. Also a strange large black bird with an orange glow around it landed to the left on the neighbour's wall. Michael looked confused at the bird and then at the man, who was strangely dressed in a black 'Nazi SS uniform' and seemed to be walking a few inches off the ground. Michael chuckled curiously with amusement; he would not have done so if he knew what circumstances were going to unfold next. This old man that Michael had seen was the same sinister ghost that was impersonating the old man 'Stan,' and the same figure that terrified Anna a few days ago. The ghost stopped and *stared* spookily and slowly in the direction of Michael.

Back in the living room Anna woke up abruptly, she could see me awake sitting beside her and she could can hear Hans' electronic instruments bleeping and squeaking from the hallway, these sounds added to her unease, making her feel more on edge. She expected and sensed like me that something was about to take place. Nevertheless we spoke a few words about 'past matters' to calm each other's minds.

Outside Michael still stared at the ghost, thinking quite innocently that it could be nothing unusual. The ghost or entity continued to glare at Michael. Without doubt Michael decided to *question* its motives. 'Who do you think you are staring at old man?' he said while giving the ghost an aggressive glance. At once the strange black bird on the wall squawked then disappeared.

'Wretched birds!' mumbled Michael. He glanced back at the old man and continued. 'You should be in bed fella! Past your bedtime in it?' The ghost smiled and its face had a sinister expression, it approached Michael methodically precise. Its features became younger and its countenance began to get bigger and bigger. The eye sockets became hollow and black and it began to mutate into a hideous creature. Michael struggled to remove his pocket torch out of his trouser pocket so he could shine a light on whatever it could be.

Hans Neily sat unnerved in the hallway examining one of the TV monitors when his attention was drawn to the electronic equipment. They started to show off crazy readings and the different needles and L.E.D. lights were going out of sync. Hans became excited about what was happening.

'Michael!' he cried. 'Quick come in here now?' There appeared to be no sign of him. Again he called out: 'Where are you?'

Michael who remained outside had now been gripped by severe fear. He shone his torch not believing what his *eyes* were witnessing into the direction of this ghost or entity. Turning behind him he shouted for 'Hans to come to his aid.' He called out again the name of 'Hans Neily' while facing back in front of him. The man ghost figure morphed into another shape, and then the entity materialized only a few feet away from Michael. He pressed the rubber button on his torch but the bulb blew up and a massive alien head with terrifying facial features - all covered with an orange illuminating light - knocked into the body of Michael. He screamed and put his hands out to protect himself. The security light from the neighbour's house immediately came on.

Anna and me heard the 'scream' from outside and we went into the hallway to where Hans was sitting. We all heard another 'scream.' My head and nervous eyes moved towards the direction of the front door entrance.

Hans became devoid of uncertainty and rose up from his seat.

'What's that shout?' voiced Anna.

'Something is starting,' said Hans. 'My instruments are picking something up.'

I'd quite had enough of this and went to the doorway to investigate. I gestured to Hans and he duly followed me.

'Anna,' I said. 'Stay where you are in the hallway, until *we* know what is unfolding outside.'

On the grass near the front of my house me and Hans were shocked to see Michael struggling with violent convulsions - the convulsions were hauling him all over the ground. Also dirt and grass stains covered his grey shirt and jeans.

'Michael!' I said shocked.

'Take this thing off of me!' yelled Michael. 'Take it off!' Suddenly he began to go into some kind of fit. Scratch marks from an invisible force ripped into Michael's torso and I noticed an orange light a few feet away from him, the same occurrence I'd witnessed on the landing window when Anna claimed she'd seen this 'Stan Personality' a few days ago. Michael then lost consciousness; in a moment he stood facing this Stan entity in a dream like state alone in a dark nightmarish oppressing passageway. Michael cried out a 'religious quotation' thinking he was dead. This infuriated the dark *Spirit* and in an instant the terrifying non-human entity flew towards Michael screaming the words:

'Stan is here! I AM A MURDERER!!!'

'Arghaaaaaaaaa,' cried Michael, before blacking out once again. Meanwhile I'd noticed the orange illumination near Michael had disappeared, but his epileptic fit continued.

'Come on! We gotta hold his mouth,' I uttered with an air of panic. 'Anything! Anything! To stop him from swallowing his tongue.' Hans nodded and grabbed a screwdriver from out of his pocket. Next we both knelt down. Hans rammed the handle of the screwdriver between Michael's teeth while I tried my best to restrain my friend's uncontrollable arms.

'I can't hold,' I said. 'I can't hold him much longer.' I swiftly looked at Hans, waiting for an idea.

'Move him onto his side!' The big man said with gasps of breath. Hans put his large lightly scratched hand over Michael's convulsing chest to try and stabilize this medically dangerous situation. The indoor lights to my embarrassment came on from the next-door neighbour's semi-detached house, and I could see Carol's face peering through the pulled back patterned curtains. I knew we had to drag Michael into the house before someone called the police.

Anna heeded my 'order' and stayed in the hallway for a few minutes despite the pandemonium unfolding with Michael; she could see Hans and myself trying to help and restrain my friend. Thinking that maybe she could help the situation and against my advice, Anna edged a few steps to go outside. Then suddenly a small silver spark raised skywards from Hans Neily's Diode machine - making her stop firmly. She nervously faced towards the other electronic instruments and they were reacting wildly.

Next she heard a massive bang that made the whole house vibrate. She could hear Hans and my voice reverberating from outside. At that moment one of the video cameras slowly moved direction, making a loud whirling sound. She gazed up and blue sparks, plus a kind of silvery glitter dust began falling from upstairs. Anna became distressed, it affected her voice and she found it hard to swallow any saliva, her mouth by this time felt completely dry.

In fear Anna whispered: 'Andrew, be quick. Hurry up, hurry up!' The words fixed in her consciousness for a moment. My wife shivered and her eyes glanced towards *one* of the televisions, blackness filled the screen. Then inexplicably the screen brightened. She shook her petite head slowly side to side and started to nervously breathe. Surprisingly, a blurred dark face formed on the television screen.

'Oh no. Please no!' mumbled Anna in a strained tone. The image on the TV screen smiled before melting away into the dark snowy mush of the screen.

Outside Michael had come out of his fit. Hans and me managed to pull him up and tried to make our way back into the house. Carol and John came in a forthright fashion out of their neatly pruned place of abode to find out what all the commotion was about. I made some phoney excuse about 'Michael suffering an epileptic fit and he just needed to take his medication.' Hans intervened with a 'swear word' in their direction and Carol stormed back into her house followed closely by John. I protested to Hans that he'd not been very diplomatic with the term of 'word' he used, but I was in no mood for an argument. I just wanted to get all of us back inside.

We struggled through the front opening and then slammed the makeshift door hard behind us - taking a few unsteady steps into the hallway. I could see Anna seemed tense and she kept shaking like a leaf, so I left Hans to carry Michael while I went over to my wife.

'What's wrong?' I asked while trying to fill my lungs with short bursts of air.

Anna stared at the television. 'I saw a *face* on the *TV*.'

I looked hard at the television but could only see a dark picture coming from one of the video cameras near the landing. I then examined one of the video machines - the indicators displayed 0000. Consequently nothing had been recorded.

Hans helped Michael further into the hallway and made him sit down on his chair facing the television monitors. Michael's jeans were ripped and so was his grey shirt after being torn open due to the fracas, which caused insult to his usual pride. To complete the misery his battered featured face seemed to be shrouded in a 'white death mask' with blood seeping from a gashed lip, caused by the overuse of Hans Neily's screwdriver. Also Michael's breath was weak and he was twitching and quivering.

I clapped my hands and touched Anna. 'Go get a glass of water for my friend,' I asked. My wife gradually did as she was told. Hans and me examined Michael to pinpoint any other injuries; he murmured a few in cohesive sentences to our questions and then coughed gruffly.

Anna came from the kitchen holding a glass of cold water and passed it towards Michael's shaking hands. He took a few sips swallowing the liquid in large gulps.

'What went on out there?' said Anna.

'You wouldn't want to know,' replied Michael in a barely recognizable tone. 'I think I'm going mad with all this whole business.'

'Are you more rational now?'

'Anna I'm—' He paused before continuing - stammering the first few words. 'I—I'm...scared. There is something I have just seen. Something...something terrible.'

Hans asked a question fuelled with speculation. 'What did you witness? There definitely was something happening because of the readings my oscilloscope green wave machine kept out putting.'

'First of all,' replied Michael. 'It, or whatever "it" was, had the appearance of an old man - perfectly normal apart from the way it walked. Then it changed into something horrifying, a transfiguration of evil.'

Anna started to panic. 'Oh my God! You have seen him. You've seen the same old man! Andrew, there's evil here! We've got to leave this place. Please—' Suddenly Anna was interrupted by a slow bang, she shuddered in fear, the bangs began to quicken and become more audible. The sounds were coming from the kitchen. I turned my head quickly in fright to the direction of the *noises*. I gritted my teeth and my face showed tension and anxiety.

'Jesus Christ!' I bellowed. 'What is going on now?'

'It's coming from the kitchen,' said Hans.

Hans and myself instantly headed to the kitchen doorway. I briefly stopped though and hastily shouted a few instructive words to my wife. 'Anna, stay where you are! Stay with Michael, and take care of him. Don't move, you hear!'

I ran into the kitchen but suddenly everything became silent. Then without warning the electric cooker began smashing from side to side and moving forward violently on its own - followed by numerous plates and cups rising up into the air and smashing against the tiled wall.

'This is certainly poltergeist activity,' said Hans while a plate flew past his head. 'I haven't witnessed this type of activity since I investigated the San Diego poltergeist case in 1982.'

'Poltergeist! A noisy spirit! That's great,' I said. Before I could say anything else a couple of large knives rose out of the sink and stayed in mid air for a couple of seconds, they were then catapulted forward causing them to fly towards myself and Hans.

'Look out!' I shouted. We both ducked and the knives embedded themselves with great force into the wall behind us. Hans got up and witnessed the cupboards being wrenched off the wall. There were numerous orange sparks now coming from the ceiling. I glanced up and could see the sparks 'burning letters' to form a *phrase*.

'Can you see them letters appearing,' I said.

'With complete distinction,' replied Hans.

The letters being mysteriously formed on the ceiling created the words, *Natasha Is In The House*. I was just about to speak again when the kitchen fluorescent light blew up. At that moment I felt something jump onto my back, pinching me.

'Hans! Christ!' I yelled. 'There's something on my back.'

The big man looked hard in the darkness, and could make out an image forming. A strange yellow and orange light began to form into a cat.

I began vigorously moving my arms in an attempt to beat this thing away.

Hans exclaimed, 'It's a cat. I don't believe it. A full materialization has appeared.' He was about to put his hand near it when suddenly the electric cooker came crashing toward us. The thing or whatever it was then jumped off me and I took a hold of Hans' shoulder. The unexplained disturbances forced both of us to fall out backwards from the kitchen with the door slamming violently shut, this had been caused by the weight of the cooker rattling against it.

Michael and Anna were stood in the hallway and could hear the banging and commotion coming from the kitchen. Anna took a few steps and thought about going to see for herself the damage that was being caused, but Michael grabbed her and pulled her beside him. Then she shivered as the atmosphere changed into something cold and oppressive. She glanced around in a highly sensitive fashion when all of a sudden the noises from the kitchen stopped. Anna stood completely still.

'Remain here with me. Please!' said Michael. He was just about to voice another word when electronic mechanism noises hummed - interrupting him. Then one of the video cameras began vibrating up the stairs wall; this caused him to become rigid. A peculiar silence filtered through the air. For a moment Michael and Anna felt relieved, then suddenly one of the video cameras exploded in an orange flash and bang. They became terrified and clung to each other in fright. Pieces from the camera fell down the stairs. Hans and myself entered the hallway after our fracas in the kitchen, and Hans could see his electronic graph reacting crazy - along with the oscilloscope and other various instruments. I stood by the side of Anna, who had by now had released her grip from Michael, and we watched the unfolding events. There was then a loud burst of radio white noise coming from Hans' Diode machine, and the big reel-to-reel tape machine came on by itself. He rushed to his chair and sat down in front of the makeshift table. Me, Anna and Michael gathered slowly behind the big man. Natasha the electronic ghost came through and began to speak in a hissing robotic voice.

'Good evening Dr. Hans Neily.' This was followed by a deviant pause. 'Have you come to torment me?'

Hans had intent overriding confidence about himself. He replied back to Natasha in an obscure 'ancient dialect.' Michael and I found this course of action confusing. Natasha answered back in German, with a slight delay after each word.

'Ich...Liebe...Dich...Einer...Zimmer...Zim.'

Michael interrupted. 'What is it saying! What does it mean?'

'Quiet!' shouted Hans. He waved his left hand furiously to display his annoyance.

'Fruchbar! Fruchbar!' Natasha pronounced. 'Where I inhabit people are in pain. I live. I live. Andrew Stein I am in your house. I am standing by the side of you.' I felt an icy cold sensation trickle down my neck when these words were spoken.

'I don't like this at all,' I said. 'The whole bloody thing. It's ghosts at the windows, waiting to come in.'

Hans addressed my concerns. 'Let me deal with it. I beg of you.'

I became justifiably annoyed - after all - the events were happening in my house. I wiped away at my face, and then Anna grasped my hand, which gave me some reassurance. Consequently my temper eased and my irritation faded for the time being.

Natasha asked a few more untrue personal questions but Hans did not answer. His course of action seemed to enrage this ghost or entity.

'You will answer me!' Natasha demanded.

Hans and all of us remained quiet. The hissing robotic voice became even angrier. 'ANSWER ME!'

'I will not!' replied Hans. He then proceeded to give his own forceful backlash. 'You have no right to belong on this earthbound plane. I command you and any other presences to retreat back to the spiritual bridge you have crossed. And end the intrusion of this astral plane.' A few audible sounds that I can only describe as animal replied back, followed by a name clearly spoken:

Wolfgang Peterson Is Here.'

Hans dismissed this name with contempt. 'My friend is dead! Don't pretend to impersonate him Natasha. Go back I—I...co— command you.' The last sentence Hans uttered seemed to have a core of indecision about it. It obviously was an unwise thing to show - as his face got struck by an invisible hand - sending him spinning backwards and tipping the large man out of his chair. Me, Anna and Michael knelt down to see if he had been hurt. Hans pushed us away and yelled up towards the ceiling.

'I command you to leave this place! Or I will drive you out in my own way!' We then heard a massive charge of static electrical power erupt from the Diode machine on the table before Natasha 'screamed words' with intense venom and hate.

'HEAR I HANS NEILY! And your compatriots! Your rancid compatriots standing by your side!'

We all gazed transfixed up in the direction of the Diode machine as the voice continued to an ear piercing volume.

'You will all die! We come through the infinite ASTRAL TIMESTREAM.' A brief silence halted proceedings before we all heard one last screaming hateful group of words.

'You will all die! DIEEEEEEEEEEEE!'

Hans struggled up and pulled the one plug that supplied the main power source for the Diode machine out of the socket.

Suddenly there were a number of loud bangs coming from upstairs in slow succession. Hans got up from the floor and pushed past us. He began making his way to the bottom of the stairs. It appeared he might be inclined to progress up the steps towards my workshop. This I thought did not seem the right course of action to take. This man seemed to me to have strange ideas about the paranormal power clearly energizing throughout the house.

Anna released her hand from my grip and she and Michael started to follow Hans nervously. He turned towards them making frantic arm gestures to 'Stop!' Anna stared at his slightly bearded face and could see a massive red *mark* where the invisible hand hit him.

'No Mrs. Stein, do not move,' the big man stated with stern words. Next he uttered another instruction towards Michael. 'You must wait down here to observe, and check the rest of my electronic instruments. You have to be in unity with me. Watch the exact readings they are outputting. I've cut the power to the Diode machine, so accordingly, you will not hear any more voices.'

I pushed past my wife to strongly protest. 'That's absolute bullshit! It does not need a fucking Diode machine anymore to make contact, I know, I've seen how this thing works.'

Hans raised his voice in response. 'Don't swear at me and

question my motives! I know what I'm doing, nothing can harm us.'

'That's rubbish! It's absolute drivel.'

Michael my dishevelled friend angrily intervened. 'Andrew's right! You're out of your depth. Arsehole!'

Hans to my abhorrence went for Michael, grabbing him around the throat. Michael who'd already been through enough unfortunate action this evening kicked out hard and they started brawling on the floor.

Anna began screaming. 'Stop it! Please Stop!'

I somehow separated the brawling pair and we all began fiercely 'arguing' with one another for a minute. Our childish altercations were abruptly silenced though by a thunderous crash that came from upstairs.

'Listen! Listen to me!' exclaimed Hans while checking his watch. 'We are doing exactly what this ghost Natasha and the other entities want. It's up to us now to banish these malevolent forces, they are growing stronger, and becoming more powerful by the minute. They are feeding off our doubts and emotions. Andrew and me must face it. Now!'

'But you're—you're not going up stairs?' Anna stated with foreboding. Hans punched his black leather chair in frustration and begged us all to be silent. My doubts about Dr. Neily were becoming more profound. I think he had not experienced this kind of violent paranormal activity before. No matter how intellectually gracious he made claim to be.

Chapter 12

Natasha Materializes

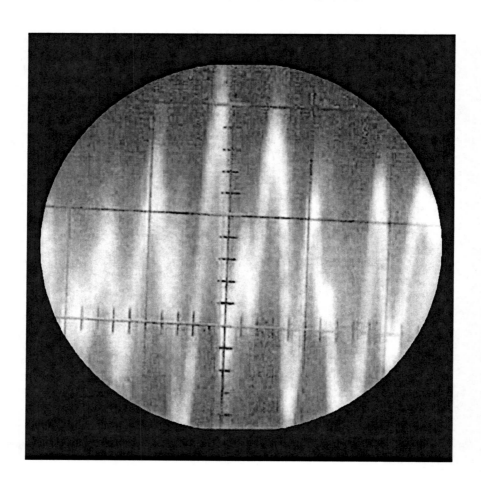

Natasha Materializes

Michael's feelings were urging him that it would be best if we all left the house and go to another location before anything else happened. Anna agreed and made her 'point' desperately known to Hans, but by now his over enthusiastic ego did not need advice. He felt a sense of pride in what he was undertaking, and seemed prepared to confront this invisible paranormal force head on. I had grave doubts; I feared that something dreadful could unfold. But there was no talking this big man out of it.

I looked at Anna while trying to hide the apprehension in my eyes. 'My dear! Let me ring a cab for you. Go round to a hotel for the night, because I don't want you getting involved any deeper. You've been mentally hurt enough.'

Anna was typically stubborn. 'I will not. I'm not leaving you in this house Andrew. If I go, then you must come with me.'

I glanced at Michael. 'Will you take my wife to your place?' Hans interrupted agitated: 'He can't go! I need someone downstairs to check the electronic graph reading - and to study what the video cameras are picking up.'

I demanded that Hans let me have a 'private word' with Michael for a moment. Finally the big man agreed to my demand. I told my friend that if things looked like they were going to deteriorate - that he take Anna and himself to my car and drive to a place of safety. Michael nodded in agreement to my request.

Abruptly Hans called out. 'Move up behind me Andrew! Follow me at once!' Slowly he began to take a few steps up the stairs - while holding an electronic indicator device that he'd kept in his pocket. I tapped Michael on the shoulder and wagged my *finger* at him to 'remember what to do if anything else happened.' I shakily took a few steps towards the stairs; Anna tugged on my shirt and she had a fearful expression.

'You are not going to do what he is telling you. I don't trust him!'

I had tense features creased on my unshaven face. 'I've got to! I created this,' I said with trepidation. 'Now I've got to try and finish what I began. I have to trust this man, even if he seems "out of his depth" with these paranormal actions occurring.'

I embraced Anna and gave her a long kiss. Then overtly I backed away, and told her to stay downstairs with Michael.

Hans again called my 'name' as he advanced awkwardly up the stairs.

I remained standing at the bottom of the staircase briefly, before I ambled up a few hesitant steps. I could see his enormous backside reaching the top so I quickened my step; I wanted to be with him when he reached the summit of the stairs.

A minute or so later we both stood on the landing. It was dimly lit due to one of the main lamps lying broken on the floor. My eyes moved nervously around, everything seemed quiet, the banging had stopped and events seemed quite normal under the circumstances. Then Hans' electronic instrument he held short-circuited and failed. He threw it to the floor in despair. At that precise moment we could hear directly in front of us the sound of someone shuffling speedily around. It seemed as if they were wearing slippers or something similar, but we could see nothing there.

In the gadget filled hallway Michael sat with some discomfort in the chair near the front of both television monitors. He curved down to the floor with hindered movement to adjust one of the main auxiliary audio cables; Anna stepped closer to Michael's position near the chair and squinted her blue eyes. One of the television's pictures began to flash with interference and jump erratically. She could just make out 'Hans Neily' and 'myself' standing on the landing. Then the snowy interference affected her normally reliable eyesight.

Michael was busy in the task of continuing to bend one of the audio cables - he cursed in dismay as he tried to adjust this lead. Anna peered at the other television and through its black screen mush some kind of transfiguration started taking the form of a ghostly face. She tapped furiously on Michael's shoulder and he jolted up with surprise. 'What is it?'

Anna pointed to the television screen for a moment with the ghostly face appearing on it. 'What's that? On the screen,' she uttered with a nervous crack in her voice. 'I saw it earlier.'

Michael turned to the television and was astonished at what his eyes portrayed to him. The ghostly face developed with a defining clarity, it had the features of a woman. Anna put her wedding ringed hand up against her mouth and gasped. Michael had seen enough and he began to shout anxiously up the stairs.

'Hans! Andrew! One of the cameras is picking something up,'

Hans shouted back strongly. 'By grief man! What is it! What are you seeing?'

Michael studied the image of the face, which had an evil grin on it. It seemed to obscure and blur out of focus for a moment, but he could just make out a hand moving its six, rather odd looking fingers in some kind of *unknown sign*. The television picture then became perfectly clear, revealing the woman's face making word-like pronunciations with its lips. The lips moved in a slow methodical fashion.

'Christ! "Its" a woman!' shouted Michael franticly. 'The face of a woman.' His next words came out in a nervous shriek. 'My God! It's right in front of you two.'

I stepped forward, waited a second, before I stared hard into the dim light in front of me. Next I whispered: 'I can't see a damn thing!'

Suddenly the window near the landing where Hans and me were situated began to slowly have a large crack appearing on it. This was followed by banging sounds and 'hissing voices' all originating from within *my* workshop.

'I don't like this,' I said. 'Lets get the hell out of here!'

Anna in a torrent of emotion desperately shouted from downstairs. 'It's there! We can see it on the *T V* monitors.' Anna and Michael's eyes stared hard as the face began to slowly disappear into the mush of the television screen interference.

Back on the landing Hans and me were trying to catch a glimpse of this mystery face that one of the video cameras supposedly picked up. Everything then seemed to go quiet, and there was only an eerie silence. All the sounds that we had previously heard in front of us had ceased. The oppression and drama of the whole situation made my body ache, but the worst was yet to come. Before I could say anything a sort of silvery glittering dust started to appear high in the air in front of us. It then brightened the whole of the landing with a spooky dull white light. I watched in disbelief at what was happening. 'What's going on now Hans? You're the damn expert!'

Hans looked in amazement at what began unfolding in front of his bloodshot eyes. He quickly took out his spectacles and put them on to gain a more purposeful view. 'I have no idea Andrew,' he murmured. 'I've never seen anything like this in my thirty-two years experience of research.' Hans turned away from this dust and bellowed excitedly down to Michael and Anna.

'Are you two watching this downstairs?'

In the hallway Michael stared inflexibly at the television monitor, he tried flicking the switches on the silver control panel with his fingers. He desperately sought to obtain different camera positions, but no matter how he tried - he witnessed nothing. Anna's eyes gazed hard at the television screen, trying to pick out any shapes that might have been missed by Michael, but she too could not see any mysterious images. Michael shouted back in reply to Hans' question. 'I'm getting absolutely FUCK ALL!'

Up on the landing we were still transfixed by this spooky light. Suddenly the bright glittery dust began to form into a shape, it brightened and slowly materialized into a beautiful angelic woman figure. I glanced towards Hans for reassurance about what we were supposed to *do* next. But he seemed to be on another planet, he stood frozen to the spot observing in sheer absolute amazement this paranormal display he was witnessing. I glanced back at this mysterious figure and began to hear a quiet clicking sound in my left ear, my body then began to feel some kind of invisible force pull me forwards. My breathing was slowing down and faintness enveloped me. I stepped forward; I seemed to be losing control due to this kind of hypnotic trance which had taken me over. The strange ghostly figure beckoned me towards it. The clicking sound in my ear got louder and I wanted to get out of the house, but I was unable to move in the direction my brain wanted me to. I felt that some kind of paranormal force had started entering me. I seemed devoid of pain, as I could not feel Hans' finger poking me. Hans furiously continued digging into my arm to bring me out of this trance. He was shocked and frightened for only the second time in his life, the first being escaping from the Amazonian Indians in his search for the ill fated *Colonel Percy Fawcett* expedition. Hans tried desperately to haul me back. At that moment the big man felt two hard slaps hit his already red face, this action knocked his professor like spectacles off onto the floor. He flailed his right arm in front of him to try and defend himself from this invisible force. But he was attacked with *blue flashes* that were coming from out of thin air.

Anna shouted upstairs for me to answer her. Hans tried to 'console my wife on my behalf' but he got *hit* in his stomach by a few powerful punches. He doubled up in pain and just managed to shout a few words in my direction.

'Andrew! Don't! Don't provoke it!'

Suddenly all the video cameras that remained on the wall down the staircase began to spark and rattle. Anna rushed away from Michael and 'screamed' upstairs for me. At that moment a number of tiny electrical bangs that sounded like gunfire could be heard, these were followed with bright electrical flashes. Anna ran back to Michael in fear, Michael, who was watching the television monitors, jumped and screamed due to the cameras exploding. He desperately shouted in a helpless tone.

'I'VE LOST ALL THE PICTURES!'

Anna screeched in terror. 'For gods sake! We have got to get out of here!' She gazed trance like towards the front door as a means of escape from the terror that now filled the house.

Our next-door neighbours, John and Carol, had come out of their house, and also there were various other people from the village who'd been woken by the strange bangs and commotion that came from my place of residence. Another bunch of sounds filled the air; it was if a gun had been fired in quick succession. John ran into his house and called the police, as he feared someone had been shot. At the Police Station a clerk received the call and automatically initiated 'an armed response' team to immediately go to the scene.

Back on the spookily lit landing Hans made a desperate lunge to try and drag me to the floor. He moved forward to try and catch me when suddenly a blinding white and blue flash emanated with great speed from this angelic apparition figure. I felt an enormous burst of energy pass through my body at that moment, this sent me falling forward and my head hit the carpet floor. I was knocked out and unaware of the events which followed. The ball of light continued on slamming right into Hans' big chest.

'ARGHHHHHHHH!' he screamed, and waved his hands in front of him frantically.

Michael and Anna again shouted upstairs for us all to 'get out of the house.'

Hans began to be pushed backwards. He tried with all his strength and weight to fight this force, but an invisible hand gripped the back of his hair and he levitated off the floor. Then Natasha's ghostly voice creepily entered his ears.

'Hans Neily. You left Wolfgang Peterson your friend to die! He suffers in torment due to your selfish action during the Fawcett expedition.'

Hans exclaimed with fury and terror. 'That's not true! Shut up! I demand you. Now leave this place and return back to your own damnation world of perverse electronics!'

There was then another burst of energy from the angelic ghostly figure, which hit Hans full in the face breaking his nose, the enormous power threw him backwards quickly and he crashed violently through the landing window. He let out one last desperate 'scream' calling my name: 'ANDREW!' Before he fell out of the shattered window opening and hit the ground outside the house with a loud thump. A thunderous vibration and a massive explosive bang caused sections of the walls to crack;

pictures and pieces of plaster subsequently dropped to the floor around the house.

Back in the hallway, Michael decided to do what I had asked him, as events had now turned violent and it was too dangerous - so he barked at Anna to 'follow him out of the front door.' Michael had just been about to stand up from the chair in front of the television monitors when he heard a loud high pitched buzzing in his ears; the level of the sound became intolerable. He screamed at Anna to 'make for the front entrance.' Michael put his hands over his head and yelled in pain due to this noise in his ears. He peered hard at the electronic control panel one last time. There were little orange and yellow static sparks rising up into his face causing it to sustain many cuts.

'Anna!!!' yelled Michael. 'Cover your eyes from the lights! Run! For godsakes run!' Anna's eyes glared at Michael's face and she could see the cuts were now bleeding profusely. Then one of the television screens started to crack and electric charged smoke came out of it. Anna pulled on Michael's torn shirt in panic to try and help him get to the front door. Just when she did this, a massive blue powerful spark *stuck out* at her from thin air, accompanied by an electronic 'ghostly sounding scream.' It lifted my wife off the floor due to the power and sent her crashing along the hallway. She let out a shrieking cry before she lost consciousness.

Instantly Michael freaked out, and began shouting and bawling. Then the other television flashed and sparked - and an orange beam reached out from the tape recorder hitting Michael. He clutched his chest and fell to the floor unconscious.

Outside, Hans was lying on the ground near the front of the house, his large body had glass all over it and blood was dripping from his head and mouth. John and Carol went to his aid. John held his arm checking for signs of life. 'Damn it! There is no pulse.' He immediately performed mouth to mouth, this did not work, so he began thumping hard on Hans' chest to try and make his heart beat.

Some other people gathered round in a morbid fascination due to all the events. Their heads moved up in the direction of the top windows of the house, they could see little orange flashes and the front windows starting to crack. John turned Hans with a degree of difficulty onto his side to see if that would help him in some way. But it was too late - he was totally dead. Carol had a shaken facade on her face. 'How long! How long,' she said, 'will it take for the police to arrive?'

'It's armed response! So they should be here soon.' Abruptly John coughed, and began shaking. He shook his head to regain self-control and began wiping dirt from his arm. Next he brought out a handkerchief and began to dab the blood from Hans' pale face.

Without warning another ear piercing bang came from the house. 'Listen! Carol. Get away from this place?' John then shouted at the small crowd of people gathering nearby. 'Stand back. For Christ sake! You wanna get hurt.'

Suddenly in the distance police sirens screamed with urgency.

Upstairs on the landing I lay dazed and motionless on the floor. I tried to speak but could only whisper a few incoherent words. I felt light headed and spaced out. I squinted and then opened my sore eyes. The pain in my face hurt immensely. My complexion was ashen and drawn with fear - and my nervous body was drenched in my own sweat. I looked behind me and could see the smashed landing window opening becoming encased in a thick greenish solid mist. I screamed for Anna and Michael but got no reply back. I knew I must try and get up.

Suddenly directly in front of me the colour of the lighting from the ghostly apparition turned from spooky white to a darkish grey mist. I gripped the carpet and gazed up from my low position on the floor. A dark figure then started to materialize where the angelic figure had once stood.

Outside, five police cars and a large police armed response van came to a halt by the road in front of my driveway. Four heavily armed policemen jumped out of the van and their fellow colleagues exited from their vehicles. After a few 'heated exchanges' with each other they manhandled a number of people, all in an attempt to remove the curious locals from the vicinity of my house. A makeshift taped cordon was then erected near the driveway to close off the scene to any other nosey onlookers.

Back indoors I clearly heard shouting coming from outside accompanied with the droning noises of sirens, but these were not my concern. In between flashes of luminosity I still observed this dark figure, which had completely materialized ahead of me. It seemed to have the outline of a W*oman*. It was sprinkled with a sort of glittery stardust material. It began disappearing and reappearing quickly every time it graced closer to me. I knew this force, or whatever it might be had come to attack my unfortunate *self*.

'Go away! No. NO!' I shouted terrified at it.

A foul smell filled the air. Its unpleasant aroma began to make me feel nauseous and cause my stomach to heave, I now felt I would be sick. Suddenly the ghostly dark figure appeared to be standing only a few inches away from my head. I noticed it had no legs and was levitating with immense power. Then two black leathery hands passed over my shoulder. My whole body started to vibrate and shake; next a massive kind of invisible force began pulling me upwards. I threw out my fists to try and hit out and fight this supernatural figure, but when I did this, it felt as if some kind of a material cloth tore away. Then at that moment a massive white flash of light entered into me and it lifted me totally off the ground. Now I came completely face to face with this dark figure. I *knew* exactly who this dark terrifying ghostly apparition was.

'You.' I said. I paused in shock before I repeated the name that had become embedded in my mind: 'You're, Natasha.'

In a hissing echoing voice *Natasha* replied: 'How clever of you.' It paused, and then continued in a hateful tone. 'Andrew Stein! I don't need your inferior machine anymore. I can attack the living without earthly electrical power.' Its final words ended in an exalted triumphant pitch.

Suddenly a violent icy wind enveloped the whole of the landing. Inside of me I felt enormous rage accompanied by fear, I began screaming and in a blind show of fury wrapped my hands around the neck of Natasha. I became hysterical in anger and let out a bellowing roar.

'YOU FUCKING... BITCH!'

I tried slapping my hands against this ghost or entity, but my left hand was gripped by one of Natasha's leathery arms and my wrist snapped due to the enormous strength this entity possessed, this inevitably caused a severe fracture to occur. I 'screamed out' in agony. Natasha's black hollow face began to enlarge. I could hear a policeman talking through a loudhailer outside asking for all the occupants to leave the house. Natasha's face continued to turn into something terrifying and grotesque. I tried hitting out even though my body felt intense agony. A small bone from my left wrist now protruded out of the skin due to the violence inflicted onto it. I desperately needed to escape, but this non-human entity seemed determined to kill me.

Outside the house, policemen dressed up in riot gear - and the police armed attack unit had their guns poised to shoot. Another police car screeched to a halt and four plain clothed detectives exited. John, who now stood a metre away from the police taped cordon, urged them 'not' to enter the house with guns.

Abruptly a conversation ensued between John, and a police officer called Paul Hawkings. 'You reported this incident - didn't you sir?'

'Yes,' replied John tentatively as he gazed towards an ambulance that had rolled into view. 'There is something going on in my neighbour's house. His name is Andrew Stein.'

Two paramedics near the driveway began to slowly carry *Hans Neily* with some difficulty due to his weight on a stretcher. Policeman Hawkings looked on as Hans' battered body was carried past. A paramedic glanced at Hawkings and John while shaking his head in a despondent fashion indicating their patient was *dead*, due to the injuries sustained. Next the medics walked on towards the waiting ambulance.

Another police officer continued pleading on the loud hailer for everyone in the house to 'leave' in single file fashion or they would be forced to enter.

'Do you know if your neighbour Mr. Stein has got firearms, or kept any in his house?' asked Hawkings while he made a few notes.

'I've never seen Andrew with any weapons,' said John dismissively. 'Definitely not! I don't know if he was ever interested in guns. Surely he would have told me. But there happened to be an incident a few days ago, when Anna his wife, for whatever reason continuously screamed from inside the house and Andrew assumed it might be an intruder assaulting her. We forced open the front door to try and catch this mystery assailant - but I never saw any evidence to confirm this. I searched the house thoroughly so I can vouch for that.'

Hawkings prepared to ask another question when suddenly in short succession there came the sound of brief thunder claps heading in the direction of the armed police.

'Incoming! Get down!' shouted a police officer. 'Someone's firing at us.' Two of the police car windscreens then shattered sending splinters of glass into the air.

In my house on the landing, Natasha's grip around my neck grew tighter; I began to feel myself losing consciousness. At that moment my workshop door flew open and all my equipment came flying violently out of it, this was followed by thick acrid smoke that filled the house like a dark cloud. Natasha's face then attained its full shape of terror. I tried to let out a roaring scream but the black leathery hands round my neck were squeezing tighter and my vocal chords could say nothing. Then in an instant a massive blue flash lit up the whole of the inside of the house.

Outside, the blue flash caused a thunderous enormous bang to erupt causing a few of my front windows of the house to shatter and blow outwards. Pieces of glass and other debris hit some of the people and the policemen. An officer with his gun stumbled and hit the ground and a few people screamed, dazed and confused.

Back inside Anna who lay dead still on the floor downstairs started to come round. Her eyes blinked quickly open. She could *see* smoke vividly coming from all of the electronic equipment in front of her, Michael lay unconscious a few feet away. She rose up in a disjointed fashion as the dark and smoke hindered her eyesight. The noises of the attack against me by Natasha - Anna now heard clearly. At that precise moment any power that may have been working in the house cut off.

'Andrew! Help me!' cried Anna as she fell to the floor caused by an upturned cable wrapping round her ankles. A paranormal force had done this.

Upstairs this call from Anna must have affected the entity, Natasha, and it released its grip from my neck and threw me back onto the ground. I then felt an enormous pressure push on my back; it felt as if a large man sat astride on top of me. I felt a massive slap strike me on the face causing my cheek to bleed and myself being pulled up again. I was pushed towards the landing window opening. I tried with all my strength to hold on to the stair banister, but my grip loosened due to my left wrist being useless, the fracture caused by Natasha's strength attributed to that. I knew my only chance must be to hold on for a minute longer to see if anyone could come to my assistance. At that moment the already damaged front door came crashing open and in came policemen with torches and in riot gear screaming their various 'orders.' Anna let out a 'loud scream' before two policemen ran over to her in an attempt to pull her out of the house. Another officer shone his torch on Michael who remained on the floor breathing heavily. Michael's body lay covered in pieces of copper wire and other debris, his face was white, and his hands were red and cut. Anna grabbed one of the policemen before going into shock.

'Please! It's Andrew. He is upstairs,' she pleaded. Policeman Hawkings and a colleague went to the bottom of the stairs and shone their bright torches upward, their eyes staring hard. They could just make out a *dark image* smiling from the top of the stairs. This became their first glimpse of Natasha, thinking it might be me and their skeptic ignorance clouding their judgment they screamed:

'Mr. Stein! The games are over! OUT! OUT!' Then with bated breaths they took a few steps unwisely onto the staircase.

At that moment my grasp of the stairs banister released and a powerful force sent me in the direction of the landing window opening. The thick greenish solid mist that filled the space instantly melted away. I continued falling backwards, my right hip caught the side of the window frame and instead of falling directly out and to almost certain death; I spun round once and struck a large tree near the left hand side of the house. I heard a few shocked shouts coming from the people who were standing near my driveway when the tree broke my fall. I hit the damp grassy ground though with a sickening thump to lengthen my agony.

Back within the image of the ghost N*atasha* disappeared from the view of Hawkings and his colleague. At that split second both the policemen's torches blew up and a blue powerful beam of light from where Natasha once stood thrust into them, forcing them back down the stairs. Anna tried to get away from a burly policeman who'd been restraining her and she began screaming. Suddenly smoke could be seen coming from upstairs and one of the television monitors in the hallway also reached up in flames. Hawkings turned to his other colleagues and frantically shouted for everyone to: 'GET OUT AT ONCE!'

John my neighbour gestured furiously and shouted from the front of the house for Anna - as he could see me lying injured on the ground. The other policemen who were in the house managed to drag Michael up and heave him out of the main entrance. At that moment the hallway erupted in fire and thick black charred smoke began pouring from the kitchen.

Chapter 13

The Final Conclusion

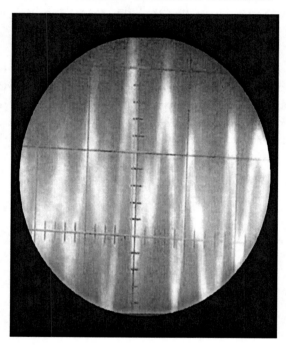

The Final Conclusion

Outside my body doubled up as I lay groaning in pain. My hip hurt immensely and in the corner of my eye I saw a paramedic pulling out some kind of oxygen mask. The different voices of strangers who I did not recognize resonated through my eardrums. I gasped for breath and began to cough up blood. The voices around me were becoming more desperate and I feared I might die. Anna rushed through the front door entrance and witnessed me lying on the ground near a tree. In emotional turmoil she ran to be near her husband, pushing various people out of the way. She knelt slowly by the side of me and placed her delicate hand on my forehead, taking care not to interfere with the paramedics who were busy working on my injuries. A few people gathered around and Anna clenched my hand delicately. The disorientated Michael made his way slowly through the mob and went to the side of Anna. Michael glanced back at the house for a moment, a damaging fire had now taken hold and "it" was devoid of any mercy. My friend put his left hand up to his eyes, bowed his head and sobbed profoundly due to the stress of the whole night. A fire engine's siren could be heard approaching amongst people's murmuring. And John and Carol were debating with each other about the unfolding events they'd witnessed that evening.

Suddenly policemen barked out commands. 'Will you people clear away from the area! It's not a show anymore. People are injured!'

Another bang rang out - its contribution caused the scene to became chaotic. Behind Anna the fire was unrestrained and widespread. Anna took her hand off my head and gazed back at the house, which by now was burning furiously. 'Andrew! Oh Andrew,' she wept. 'The house, we're gonna lose everything!'

At that moment I lost my breath and my lungs filled with trickles of thick clotted blood. Suddenly I blacked out, and all my pain and the noises around me disappeared. I now stood in a bluish mist; my surroundings resembled a medieval castle's chapel, lit up with burning red lanterns.

'Is anyone out there?' I said.

In a flash a woman appeared directly in front of me wearing a twelfth-century hooded brown monk's robe. Her long black hair stuck out awkwardly from the hood, she was tall, slim, and her age by my reasoning may have been about twenty-five.

'Where am I?' I asked.

She put her hands together as if to pray, then her eyes closed for a moment. When she opened them two large black empty eye sockets greeted my view. 'You are here with us...Andrew.'

'What do you mean? Here with us,' I said in fear. The burning red lanterns immediately cut out, and all that remained in their place were puffs of smoke.

Suddenly I sensed something pulling at my legs. I looked in the direction of the clouded floor and before I could react a colossal pressure forced me downwards. The fog melted away and I began falling and spinning around in complete darkness. I felt a horrendous pressure on my chest as I fell; I called out for 'help' in desperation. Through the darkness a gloomy purple light appeared, which I seemed destined to head towards. As I got closer I could see two images waiting for me. I stared hard and I could see Hans Neily, he began shouting at me.

'Andrew stay away!' he cried. 'This dimension's manipulated for evil. Hitler is here, and other despicable figures. They lurk in the electronic shadows. But Andrew! And for the love of God! Your antagonist is here, by my side. Look!'

To my horror the other person who stood with him was Natasha. *I* knew I would be definitely *dead* if I continued my descent. The spooky purple light then surrounded me. Hans stretched out his arm and I tried to grab it.

'Andrew hold on to me,' he cried. 'Hold on!'

I grasped his hand and it stopped my descent downwards. I could hear Natasha's voice 'scream my name.' In an instant the entity appeared behind *Hans Neily* and started to crush his head in between her black leathery hands. I felt the grasp from Hans lessen - and he was dragged away from me, he let out one more cry.

'Andrew! You must save yourself. Go to the light! Go into the light!'

His head then became crushed and the remnants of his spirit body or whatever its energy formation may have been fell backwards into the gloomy mist. I then started being pulled violently upwards with tremendous speed. I was now in a black tunnel with a magnificent window of white blinding light ahead of me. It began getting larger as I approached it. I turned my head to view behind me and I could see a blue sparking light with many arms coming out of it following me fast. A black hollow face popped out from this blue spectral light. It was Natasha. I gazed back towards the white light and could see my mother standing in it. Adjacent to her were a couple of my relatives and for some strange reason 'Stan', the old man who I had known all those years ago. He spoke to me.

'*...Time Is The Essence...For The Rest Of My Duties.*' His words came together in a staggered delay echo.

'Stan! All of you,' I cried. 'I don't want to die. Please send me back.'

The *words* from Stan kept repeating themselves constantly in my head. The white light began to envelop me and I felt my life force begin to drain away.

Suddenly I felt a tremendous pain rip through my head, a blinding silver flash of light followed, and I heard voices talking medical terms at a reduced speed of tone. I then breathed and came around from my unconsciousness with a massive jolt to the chest. Instantly my aching eyes opened. I now lay on a hospital bed in an 'Accident And Emergency Department'. Doctors and Nurses around me were frantically injecting me with different kinds of medicines to keep me alive. They dabbed my face and covered my mouth with an oxygen mask.

At that moment, and to my absolute horror, I witnessed to the left of me Natasha. The earthbound demon had materialized into solid form, dressed up in the guise of a green doctor's outfit. She levitated off the white surgical floor and moved closer. I grabbed one of the doctor's green jackets.

'Please don't let me die,' I begged. 'It will get me if I die.'

'Andrew! You're fine,' replied a doctor. 'We are doing our best for you. Relax. Breathe steadily. We'll make you comfortable, okay.'

A nurse hooked up some kind of monitor to my chest - which gave 'dangerous signs' about the state of my heart. I tried to cling onto the nurse; I moved my head to the left of me and felt an icy chill scratch down my neck. Anna came into the room and held my hand. 'Andrew stay with me. I love you,' she said.

Crack! I felt one of my ribs snap before a doctor injected my heart with a strong dose of adrenalin. Natasha whose appearance seemed invisible to everyone except me, glided to the side of the bed and pushed Anna away with abrupt force, making her hit the Hospital floor. A black leathery arm gripped tightly onto my chest and squeezed tightly.

'Can you see the ghost? Can you see it!' I screamed.

'It's only hallucinations. It'll go away Andrew?' uttered the nurse. Anna became uncontrollable and had to be dragged from the 'Accident And Emergency Ward'. Due to the immense pain I then let out a loud scream and the words:

'NATASHA! GO BACK TO THE WORLD OF...EVP!'

The last thing I remember before I passed out was Natasha's black hollow face *eyeing* me up and down, associated with a massive loud ghostly bang, a 'whispering voice,' and in a grand finale she vanished. My condition after that eventually seemed to stabilize. So consequently, and by a miracle, the doctors had somehow saved my life.

I do not remember anything else until I came round a few hours later in the recovery room. After that I could see two policemen standing by my bedside at different intervals, and also the loving face of Anna - but still at times I would drift in and out of consciousness.

****

The weeks that followed were traumatic for me, Michael and Anna. All of us were questioned thoroughly about those terrifying events of the night of the disturbance. The fire and the death of Hans Neily gave the police something to beat us with, though we all stuck to the 'same story' about what we had all experienced. A thorough detailed investigation by detectives and their numerous colleagues failed to bring out the correct facts. An inquest held into Hans Neily's death caused the coroner to come to the conclusion that:

Dr. Neily's Demise Had Been Caused By Misadventure and not *Manslaughter* as the prosecution hoped for. The police continued interrogating us and refused to believe our witness' statements. We all were charged with minor various offences. The only true facts that might have came out would have been from the video camera recordings made on that fateful night. But mysteriously the only one, which survived from the fire, had recorded nothing of any relevant importance. The prosecution were furious they did not have enough detailed evidence to take a stronger case to court, and miraculously we escaped with relatively minor sentences of Community Service and Fines. I felt relieved, but slightly disturbed. I blamed myself for the death of Hans Neily. It would always prey on my mind, as with other matters I'd experienced. I just could not believe how my luck prevented me from serving a term in her *Majesty's* prison.

After about nine months the police said they had 'no more need for us.' This lifted an enormous burden that hung over Anna and myself. Misfortune followed Michael though, as his Electrical Shop due to bad publicity and other factors went bankrupt. He subsequently left the country to stay with relatives in France - so we did not see him again after the police finished with us.

As for me and Anna, we reluctantly, and due to accommodation problems, rented a flat many miles away, which meant we had to leave Rex, our dog, in the kennels for a ridiculous amount of time - this contributed to a miserable existence for our pet that liked his creature comforts.

Then eventually, and due to pressing circumstances, we decided to go back to the house for the first time since *Hans Neily's* death, if only to see the true extent of what might be still left intact.

So readers, 'there' you have the full extent of my complex *story*, with the dramas and notations and paranormal intrigue.

I think it is wise to now return to the Prologue of my story. The old man Stan, in my opinion represented my youth of the 1960s, for it was his death you could say which became the ignition for my quest for proof that there is really life after physical death, though I did not realize it at the time.

1985, the year where I find myself now, would certainly be a time that I would never be able, or be allowed to forget for the rest of my life, no matter what other state of affairs might emerge. *Hans Neily's* death and the horrifying images of *Natasha* would haunt me to the day I died.

I continued to stay standing, rooted to the spot uneasily for a further couple of minutes, surrounded by my own imaginary *memories* in the fire-damaged living room. The weather became cloudier and spots of rain now tapped on the ground outside. This began causing more puddles of water to form on the charred stained carpet. My wrist, which got broken during the paranormal manifestations still ached - even after nine months, a little reminder of the unbelievable attack I was subjected to.

I heard the car horn beep a couple of times - pressed by Anna, who had no intention of coming in with me. She remained outside in the car. My weary eyes peered around one more time before I composed myself. I then walked out of the living room and stood in the wrecked hallway. I took one more glance at what was left of the damaged electronic equipment. I next made my way to the boarded up front door. After stepping outside I eventually wrenched forward this front boarded up door, firmly shutting it behind me. Then I took a few back steps away from my surroundings. I examined the outside of the house, which had been vastly damaged due to the fire. All the windows had been boarded up and parts of my house were black due to the soot and smoke. I let out a heavy long sigh. Anna wound down the passenger car window and shouted:

'Andrew. Ready to leave?'

'Yes love,' I replied in a melancholy tone.

I turned away from the house and sauntered a few steps. I gazed at the ground and noticed all the glass and debris for some reason still lying about - even after this length of time. I stopped briefly and observed a small *book* lying open on the grass. I bent down to pick it up. Its pages were waterlogged due to the weather. But the page, which had been opened by the wind and the weather stood out prominently in smudged large bold italic ink. I moved it up to my face and slowly read the words in a humble tone.

IF OUR BIRTH IS BUT A DREAM.

THEN MAYBE OUR DEATH WILL BECOME OUR

REALITY!

I, Andrew waited for a moment, before I dropped the waterlogged book to the ground and my whole persona moved slowly away. The book lay on the wet grass and the wind rustled through the remaining pages like an autumn leaf falling to the ground. I entered into the car and Anna and me took one last glance in the direction of our burnt out destroyed house - before I started the car, pressed on the accelerator, and drove off down the windswept road, unknowing if life would yield any more surprises for both of us.

THE END?

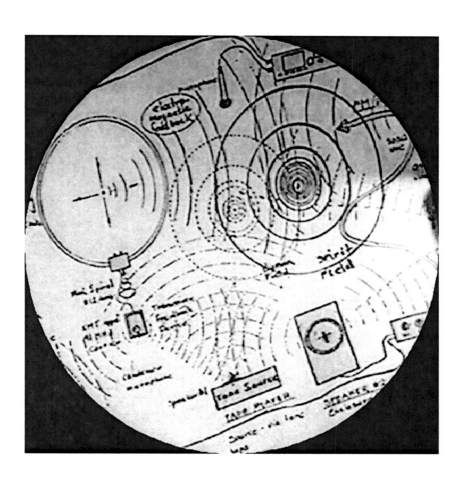

Non-Fiction Section

Electronic Voice Phenomena and Spiricom, explained by myself.

During the 1960s a Latvian scientist/psychologist living in West Germany, called Dr. Konstantin Raudive developed a technique using Tape Machines, Diodes, and Radios, to contact deceased people. Over those years Raudive amassed thousands of recorded phrases claiming to be from people who when alive - knew the experimenter Dr. Konstantin Raudive. Many emanate scientists' listened to his recordings and were baffled and unable to verify where these voices came from. *Konstantin Raudive died in 1975* leaving a legacy for other researchers to carry on his work.

How did Raudive become known to the wider world?

The Inaudible made audible'. Konstantin Raudive's original German language book of the EVP experiments he documented. This book caught the attention of the UK publisher 'Colin Smythe' in 1969. Who subsequently made available an English language version under the title *"Breakthrough"* in 1971. This gave Raudive's work much greater publicity. *Peter Bander* wrote a preface in the book about how he first heard a strange voice. The voice said. "Mach die Tur auf"- German for "Open the door". Bander immediately knew the voice was from his dead mother. Bander become convinced of the genuine nature of the 'electronic voice phenomenon' and wrote another book called:

"Carry On Talking How Dead Are The Voices".

Twelve years later a radical new way to contact the dead was unveiled by George W Meek, helped by an electronic psychic engineer called William O Neil. The year was 1982, and they had invented a weird electronic machine called *Spiricom*, short for spirit communication. This enabled O Neil to have a two-way conversation with a *Dr. Mueller,* who died in 1969. Much controversy and media interest followed, only to fall away as other scientists and experimenters were unable to replicate the results George W Meek and William O Neil had achieved through the use of their Spiricom machine.

An article, within the *Psychic News* in the early 1990s, claimed a well-known Medium called into question the true nature of some entities that spoke on 'Tape Machines, Television, Computers and other Electronic Devices.' The points raised were these really people who had died and wished to make contact? Or were they clever malevolent ghosts fooling the researchers communicating with them.

As for me I leave the reader to make up his own mind, and come to his own conclusion?

Final Thoughts

Though E.V.P. The Electronic Voice Phenomenon is a recognized science - there is a risk with this exercise. Exaggerated I must stress in this fictional book for artistic license. I strongly advise, and cannot accept any kind of responsibility if people undertake this research before reading the facts, which are essential with this process. I myself no longer engage in EVP. I've had enough proof and wish to leave it at that. I suppose it is a person's own choice and viewpoint that makes us question what becomes of us after we die. Mankind has been searching throughout the ages to find the answers to this. Through the many different religions, there are different answers to this. But the prospect of receiving Spirit messages through electronic means is an amazing development. How far it will progress, who knows? The same could go for spiritualism when it was discovered in the 1850s. But as with any kind of spirit communications, I. E., Ouija Boards, Spiritualism, and other methods - you should be highly developed, in a proper state of mind and clear your thoughts. Talk to someone in the Spiritualist community who have their own opinion in this field of contacting the deceased. Or read as many books about this process as you can. I highly recommend the books:

Breakthrough by Konstantin Raudive.

Published by *Colin Smythe*.   **ISBN 900675543**

Samuel C. R. Alsop's book.

Whispers Of Immortality.   **ISBN 0721208754**

Published by *Regency Press*. There is also plenty of information about EVP on the Internet. So you are fully aware of the whole facts that surround this paranormal, scientific subject.

My Experiences in the Science of E.V.P. 1996

After conducting my own experiments into EVP I achieved some great result. The process took some time though, it did not happen overnight. I set up the recording session one night at about 8.30pm, as this was the best time specified in the book to conduct experiments. Apparently there are a number of transmitting stations on the other side that are used by spirits to cross the bridge from their dimension to ours to make contact. That is what *Samuel Alsop* stated in his book:

"Whispers Of Immortality". At first when I started I tuned a radio to some white noise between two stations, got my minidisc recorder with microphone plugged in, and placed it near the speaker of the radio and began. For two weeks I addressed if there was any friends from the other side who would like to make contact with me. After playing back my minidisc player and listening hard to my recording session with my headphones I could hear nothing, only the hiss of radio noise. But on the twenty-fifth day of trying I listened again, and heard in the white noise mush a voice addressing me by my name speaking, *"Talk to us."* I was astonished with the results, and as the weeks progressed I got many more EVP messages, some saying: *"We are in the room"*. *"I can see you"* and some making comments about what I was doing during a recording session.

Some other messages I received were in German and other foreign languages though, which I could not understand, this made it even harder for me to respond to what I was hearing. Another night I'd been eating an apple before I began a recording session, when I played the minidisc player back an hour or so later I heard a EVP message reply, which made me chuckle a bit: *"Apple give me a bit."* E.V.P. phenomena is something that I can't explain. It is a genuine science that cannot be dismissed. Even though when I have talked to some psychic mediums, they have different views about the subject over here in England. Some have been positive, while others have told me that you only get bad spirits coming through, and other comments that border on the extreme, I suppose you get different views in all walks of life.

Konstantin Raudive's book "Breakthrough", with EVP quotes from the dictators "*Lenin*," "*Stalin*," and "*Mussolini*," may have influenced the psychic mediums in their opinions, especially when: the German Dictator *"Adolf Hitler"* seemed to manifest frequently. According to Raudive the comments he documented still showed the same traits that characterized him on Earth: self-glorification (Megalomania). Various voice examples recorded by Raudive seemed to indicate that the dimension Hitler now inhabits is a direct reaping of what has been sown while alive on earth.

Mediators:
These are a Spirit entity that helps in the link up process in EVP. If using the radio frequency method, I.E a radio tuned to white noise. A number of transmission stations exist in the beyond. Goethe Bridge, Kelpe, but the main one seems to be Radio Peter.

Raymond Cass, highly respected UK EVP experimenter achieved some amazing results with this method. His EVP messages received were on a par with Raudive's.

There are a few methods for taping spirit voices. I myself used a radio tuned to white noise on the UHF frequency and had a Sony minidisc player or tape cassette recorder with stereo microphone placed up against the radios speaker. Then I started a recording session by giving the time and date, and asking if any friends would like to come through. Be patient, the process can take a couple of months of recording, before eventually you should get a spirit voice coming through with a brief comment, a pair of headphones are essential as the voices to begin with can be quite hard to detect through the radio interference. Other people use different methods. There is plenty of useful information and technical tips on EVP websites, which give a more detailed instruction for this process. As a footnote the common computer program used by the majority of researchers these days to analyse the recordings is Cool Edit. It enables you to reverse, compress and numerous others effects to help the human ear adapt to hear the spirit voice more clearly.

(Update)

I have found though that the 'Mixcraft software' is all that you will need and it is far cheaper. Also there has been a lot of information about IC recorders, I really don't like the sound results they reproduce. I've showed examples of these recordings made by experimenters, and the results obtained by others in the 1970s and 1980s and most of the feedback I got were the older recordings, were easier to hear, and did not sound like a robot in a tin bath as one engineer put it. Remember some of the best EVPs were gained by using a good quality, old fashioned - tape recorder.

Who was Colonel Percy Fawcett?

Colonel Percy Fawcett, 1911. Picture courtesy *Fortean Picture Library*

Fawcett was born in England in 1867.

He enlisted in the British army in his youth and served in various countries. Fawcett always had an interest in the paranormal, and read a number of occultist magazines.

Shortly after the end of World War I he read a report of a 1753 expedition, which had gone into the jungle of the Amazonian Rainforests, looking for a secret city that was supposed to hold many amazing treasures. The advanced civilization were said to be highly intelligent, and may have even been descendents from the lost city of

Atlantis. This story fascinated him, and the mystique and secrecy appealed to his adventurous nature. In 1925, he made arrangements for an expedition into the South American jungle to bring proof back to the outside world - of this mysterious civilization.

Fawcett and his party were poorly supplied when they entered into the Amazon basin, they headed north to Baccari, and then further east, making camp at a spot called, *'Dead Horse Camp.'* The Colonel made an average entry in his diary about, eating, and the bothersome insects. This was his last message to the outside world, as neither him nor his party would ever to be seen again. Because he was not supposed to return until 1927, no undue concern was expressed.

In 1928, an expedition party from the USA led by *George Dyott*, set off in search of the Fawcett mission. They got to *'Dead Horse Camp'* and met some local Indians, who gave a rather whimsical story that the Colonel had gone further into the jungle. Dyott seemed convinced that Colonel Fawcett and his researchers had fallen prey to vicious Indians.

It was nearly twenty years later that *Edmar Morel* went into the Amazon to see what really had happened to Fawcett. After two days he encountered the Kalapolo tribe about nine miles from Dead Horse Camp. Morel managed to extract a confession from the Kalapolo chief who admitted the Colonel and his party had been speared to death, some remains were given to the party to provide proof of the story. A few months later Morel managed to get the remains examined by a pathologist in London. The pathologist compared them with the Colonel's medical details, and found them not be Fawcett's.

Maybe the final conclusion to the story may lie with the well-known medium *Mrs. Nell Montague. In 1951 some family relatives handed her a scarf worn by the Colonel. Using psychometry she immediately had a trance vision of Fawcett and the party being savagely attacked and killed, then their bodies being thrown into a lake.*

A book published by Fawcett's son in 1955 called *Exploration Fawcett*, was a collection of his fathers notes, and stories. And is the last known book published about the Colonel.

I myself put a reference to *Colonel Percy Fawcett* in this book:

The Electronic Ghosts.

A stage play was made about Fawcett by *Misha Williams*, a director and writer, called AmaZonia, and staged in the West End in London, he had access to many secret papers held by the Fawcett family, and even himself went to the spot where the Colonel was last seen.

I have always found the story about Fawcett intriguing, though it is irrelevant to EVP. Maybe though, someone has obtained an EVP message after going into the Amazon jungle armed with a tape recorder? And then disappeared!

By the way that idea has been copyrighted!

Recommended reading:

Cummings. G. The Fate of Colonel Fawcett

(Aquarius Press, London 1954)

THE ELECTRONIC GHOSTS *new paperback edition*

Disguise Books. UK © 2008

A Disguise Book Publication

CPSIA information can be obtained
at www.ICGtesting.com
Printed in the USA
LVOW07s1731071017
551595LV00019B/330/P